SPLEEN

SPLEEN

edited by

MICHAEL BLACKBURN

SUNK ISLAND PUBLISHING
LINCOLN

SPLEEN is issue 10 of *Sunk Island Review*
published by Sunk Island Publishing 1995.
Copyright © this collection, Sunk Island Publishing 1995
Copyright © the authors 1995

EDITOR Michael Blackburn
PRODUCTION John Wardle
COVER DESIGN Geoffrey Mark Matthews
ASSISTANT EDITORS Sylvia Blackburn, David Lightfoot

distribution by
Central Books
99 Wallis Road
London E9 5LN
(tel. 0181 986 4854)

ISSN 0955-9647
ISBN 1 874778 25 6

All submissions (including those from literary agents)
should be accompanied by stamped addressed envelopes
or International Reply Coupons, otherwise they will
not be considered.

SUNK ISLAND PUBLISHING
P. O. Box 74
Lincoln LN1 1QG
England
(E-mail: 100074. 140@compuserve.com)

CONTENTS

ΜΗΙΝ ΑΕΙΔΕ ΘΕΑ ΠΗΛΗΙΑΔ ΕΩ ΑΧΙΛΛΗΟΣ
ΟΥΛΟΜΕΝΗΝ . . .

Sing, goddess, of the destroying spleen of Achilles, son of Peleus...
ILIAD I

GO TELL THE HONEY ANT

Ken Smith

The scavenger ants trek through the forest,
each day an exact slice of the compass.
They eat everything and they spare nothing
in that sector. They are out there,
I hear them with their black flags.

There are the slaves and there are the slavemakers,
toughs who spray propaganda substances
turning their victims onto each other,
and they make off with the eggs. These are the slaves.
They do all the work around here.

That's how it is in the ant universe.
Nothing can change it. So how would you like
to be pumped up into a bag of glucose and water
hung from the ceiling against lean times?
Upside down. That's some career plan.

As for the bear grubbing in the bleak winter
of the bears, he's not interested in this
but in the rare sharp sweetness on his tongue.
He blinks. If I were you the bear in me says
I'd stick to sweet things, especially honey.

PART OF THE CROWD THAT DAY

Ken Smith

They watched the pilgrims leave for Santiago
gawping by the roadside. In the harbour
watching the boats gather they knew something
was afoot, so many horses and these armed men.
Mostly it was all difficult to believe.
They watched the stones rise in the cathedral.
They watched the stars. They watched winter
follow summer and the birds fly south again.
They watched the thieves carted up the road
to Tyburn and the beggars whipped through town.
They were townsfolk, craftsmen, shopkeepers,
the labouring poor who came in from the fields.
They watched the witches burn, the heretics.
They watched the ships leave for the Americas.
They were on the bridge at Sarajevo the first time.
They saw. They wondered. They shouted
burn her, hang him, slaughter the Albigensians.
They are the onlookers, the crowd a gasp runs
mouth to mouth through down the grumbling street
as Marie Antoinette goes by, and this time
they are shouting for her head. There goes
the Iron Duke, there the beaten Corsican,
and this the little father of all the Russians,
this the firing squad. They were on the hills
looking down on burning Rome, and still around
when Il Duce came to town, and how they cheered.
They gawp at the hungry, they gawp at the dead.

In the end they are not spared. In their turn
everything happens to them. Of any half dozen
one has a secret vice, one an incurable disease,
one a deep faith in God and the rest don't care
one way or the other. But they saw it happen.

MAN IN THE FRAME

Ken Smith

It was early evening, we were on the bus into town, me and the wife of those years. The then wife. To the pictures, I don't recall what, anything but The Sound of Music. Anything but The King and I.

This was a long time ago: the sunset falling over the city, the last light collapsing through the buildings, the bus picking up and setting down on the long slope down through Chapeltown, the conductress at the bell. She, the then wife, with our young daughter and I, lived in a third floor rented flat. I was a young teacher. She didn't get out much. So tonight someone was baby sitting, and we were going out.

We were sitting in the inside facing seats, just by the platform. The other passengers were the usual passengers, minding their own business, we minding ours: a girl with her boyfriend, man with newspaper, woman with pink hat, mother with child, man with crutch. The bus stopped. A man got on. He was carrying a full size heavy looking white painted door, with a doorknob and a letterbox and a keyhole and the number 57 on it, and a square cut in the centre where a pane of glass would go. He sat facing us on the opposite inside seat, placing the door upright in front of himself, so all that was visible of him were his fingers as he gripped it and his face looking out through the window, and in that way we went into town.

Nothing odd about it. He'd bought a door, a second hand door, or salvaged it from a site or a skip, or picked it up from a mate's. He was taking it home, where he'd fix it in the space of his own front door, changing the number to his own, and putting in a square of glass, frosted perhaps or even leaded glass, a Dutch windmill say or a ship with billowing sails or squares of blue and red and yellow. Nothing odd in it at all.

Presumably we went to the pictures, we probably walked around the city centre looking in the shops, looking at clothes and shoes, that sort of thing. She was very keen on shoes, the then wife. Maybe had a drink maybe a coffee, caught the last bus home, hours later sitting in the same inward facing seats, content with our evening, let's suppose. A stop or two down the way the man with the door got on again, still carrying it: same square of glassless window, same brown doorknob, same green letterbox, same number 57, and sat in the same seat facing us, with the door to his front boots and his two hands clutching it, his face looking out through the window. As if he'd just taken his door out for the evening.

SQUADDY

Brendan McMahon

Picked up a squaddy once, near
Doncaster, a ruined country. They'd
let him loose in Scotland somewhere,
penniless, with just a knife
to get him back to barracks.
He'd lived rough, dodged farmers'
dogs across the Borders, froze
in Northumberland. A kindly
Yorkshire lady fed him for

a dead son's sake. His life
was sad, the best times spent
at Spandau guarding Hess, a
'nice old boy'. Eye contact was
forbidden. 'I looked him in the
face.' he said, ' one time: they
put me on a charge.' I dropped
him at the Cambridge turn. He
never told me what he saw.

THE BLACK MIDDENS

David Almond

A T THE END OF THOSE HUMILIATING DAYS OF RETRAINING, BODY STIFFENED FROM BENDING AT THE BENCH ALL DAY, FINGERS ACHING AND FRUSTRATED FROM THE STRUGGLE WITH tiny screws and leads and cables, fluorescent light still burning in his brain, he would take himself away through the failing light from the brightly-painted corrugated units, pass the remaining fish sheds and converted warehouses, come to the banks where saplings and flowerbeds and new-laid turf now grew, and descend from the paved quay the ladder that would lead him down to isolation, to mudflats and rocks, the scent of weed and fish and rot, the slopping of water over ancient silt,down to the Black Middens.

Black Middens. Black sediment, black rock, black river flowing past,light of the sun catching the tips of waves, glittering, showing the tumult at the centre as the tide turned. Gulls screaming there, plunging for waste. The bell of a warning buoy ringing and ringing. Occasional dinghies with flapping white sails, low-slung container boats, great ferries heading out for Scandinavia and sending their rolling wakes at him. Beyond all this the two stone piers at the mouth, the open sea, the dead still dark horizon. The sky intensified as each day closed, began to glow and burn above Newcastle to the west, and etched upon it were timbers of ancient jetties, steeples and stacks, bowed derricks and jibs, the broken roofs of workplaces, the high fences shuttering closed yards and demolition sites.

The Black Middens. Day after day he encrouched there, plunged his fingers into it and sought the secrets in its black heart.

He dreamed that the Middens would be his salvation, that in it were riches carried by water during centuries of growth and wealth and work, and laid down here as sediment. He imagined coin, cutlery, china, fragments of jewellery, the carelessly-dropped or discarded trappings of our fortunate ancestors. He turned up bottles, broken rough pottery, pebbles and rocks and shells, plastic fishboxes, tin cans, bricks and bones. And handful of the Middens' thick black element. What was this stuff? Granulated earth, coal dust, sand, grease, engine oil, rotted fish and rotted timber turned by time and water into history's indecipherable paste. It oozed through his fingers, coagulated in his pores, stained and stiffened his clothes. The profound and almost-sweet scent of it haunted him through all those days of longing. And it gave up to him nothing but frustration. Night would fall, he would retrace his steps, climb the ladder, re-enter the town, return to what he was in truth: a working man, superfluous, an abandoned builder of ships, one more piece of useless sediment. And next day he would return to the garish shed of his retraining.

Often as he shuffled back and forth upon the black, passers-by strolling on the quay above would hesitate. He heard their mutterings, their mocking laughter. In answer to their questions – What did he seek there? What had been lost? What could he hope to find? – he showed his empty hands, the yearning eyes in his darkened face, which sent them on their way. It was worse when those who knew him, those whose voices were tender, who named him, who murmured their compassion and talked of the coming dark, the dangers of water and filth. He knew that it was love they offered him, but he never raised his eyes. He knew that soon they would turn away, that he would become for them one of those helpless ones driven into madness by our shifting times. And he knew that there was truth in this: as did so many then, he had begun to remove himself from those around him, even from those he loved, in order to indulge in solitude his bitterness, his longing, his dreams.

On the final day, there were no passers-by, no questions. A group of children played up there on the quay. Old-fashioned games: chanting games and skipping games, months of the year repeated and repeated as they leapt and spun. *January, February, March, April...* The sun was golden on their upturned faces; as they ran from their line to the rope they moved from light to silhouette and back again. Their voices mingled with the bell, the gulls, the water. The sky over everything was burnished. He pressed his fingers into the black, broke the surface, went wrist-deep, elbow-deep. Found nothing. Spread his fingers wide in there, touched tiny pebbles, an edge of rock. Clenched his fists and pushed again, went deeper, leaned his body closer to this complex place. Spread his fingers, searched the dark again, heard his beating heart, his sighing breath. Nothing. The chanting of children, ringing of the bell. From somewhere within his own darkness some old friend calling for his return. Went deeper, deeper, breast pressed now to the silt, cheek resting there, arms and hands plunged further than they'd ever been. But nothing, nothing. Spread his fingers wide, muscles aching against the density, and touched, touched at last. And gripped, and held on tight, as if he had begun to fall and needed to be caught.

He clung for his life to the black earth. He reeled. What was it that he clenched within his fingers, pressed against his palm? Someone called; the children: *Mister! You all right, mister?* He didn't move. Ached to go further, head and body to enter the dark, plunge as if the earth would open like water and told him safe again. Heard from somewhere further up the river the crashing of useless buildings onto useless quays. *Mister! What you doing, mister?* He turned to them, lifted his face, groaned at them to go on with their games. Watched their leaping, the invisible turning of the rope, their interminable line, while the wheeling of the earth and sky around him come to rest again.

He withdrew himself and began to pull away the earth: great handfuls of thick stuff that he threw aside on to rocks and into water; armfuls that he heaved into heaps at his side. Water trickled into the deepening trench, and he splashed in a soup of the river and the Middens and his sweat and the blood that seeped from the lacerations on his skin. The calling inside his skull was constant now: a great roaring, men at work, voices raised in celebration of a ship's launch; the voice of his mother somewhere, his father, so many of the dead; of his children, the woman who was his wife, those he had scorned and abandoned. Voices calling him backwards, homewards. He keeled into his excavation and the light failed and more buildings fell around him and he dug. Until he touched again, when he paused, and began again more slowly, working gently to expose what lay there in the Black Middens' heart.

A fingertip, a finger, a whole hand, slick and smooth and black as the silt itself, like a crystallisation of silt. The narrow forearm, elbow, the upper arm. Skin like leather over the shrunken flesh, the hard bone. Tracks of sinew, wiry. He washed these beginnings with black water, saw by the declining light the glistening form of this body emerging at last from the dark. Continued to dig, with water and his fingertips exposed a lad who lay there so languid with one leg folded over the other, his head turned down upon his shoulder as if he were sleeping. Hair like matted silk, face like bronze, exquisite and turned towards the river. All clothing gone except the remnants of his leather boots, and in the sediment around him were metal clasps of overalls, a metal ruler, a scattering of small coins.

He paused again in his digging. He knelt at the lad's side. He saw no marks of violence, no signs of agony. He touched in his longing the cheeks, the closed eyelids, the lips, as if something here might begin to return to him all he had lost, or as if this were a saint, or some hero from another age, who had been resting and might rise again to rout our present enemies.

The light continued to fade. The children were calling again. *Mister! What you found, mister?*

What had brought this lad to this place that had held him and preserved him? Perhaps during some long-gone dusk, in the time of crowded quays and innumerable workplaces he had lost his footing, slipped into the black river, and would have been swept beneath the hulls of tugs and loaded barges to sea were it not for a turning tide that carried him to the Middens. Perhaps even as he drowned he had heard them calling into the darkness after him. Perhaps for years afterwards he had been yearned for and searched for by workmates and loved ones while he sank and silt collected over him and embalmed him and workers bustled on the quays above.

What you found, Mister?

He turned to them, tried to speak, raised his hands in bewilderment, saw them leaning on the fence, stepping down on to the ladder. He knelt again, spread his arms, reached into the silt again, and after the struggle the lad came out so easy, with a gentle sucking sound, water running fast to fill his space. The lad was light and pliant. He rested the head against his breast. The limbs hung loosely from his outstretched arms. He stood up, stepped up from the trench.

What is it, mister?

They had come down from the quay to the Middens. They stood before him, eyes wide and scared and glowing like water. Blackness spattered their ankles and calves. He held the ancient drowned lad before them, could say nothing to them. Between them, already the excavation was being silted again: trickling water, gently collapsing ground.

Who is it, mister?

They whispered now, edged closer, held each other tight, imprints of their feet in the opened earth.

He held the lad, said nothing, and the tide turned, the river was red as molten steel, the banks and the city were black as silt. His skull was silent as the riversides all around. Felt the lad's cheek against his cheek, the hair like silk, felt his own tears running.

A dark-haired boy reached out, touched the lad's shoulder, his drooping arm. Came in close to look upon the ageless face. Touched again: the lips, the cheek. Looked up. The bloom of his white face, black gap of his questioning mouth:

Who is it, mister?

No answer.

Wake him up, Mister.

The boy reached out and touched again, held the lad's shoulder, shook him.

Go on. Wake him up.

They waited. They waited for the lad to stand before them on the black earth, with open eyes, with the evening light gathering around him. They waited for the moment when he stretches out his hand, is about to speak…

Together they watched, then gazed into each other's empty eyes. He turned, with the lad in his arms and the boy at his heels. He walked to the edge of the Middens, the confluence of sediment and water. Feet slithered here where the nature of the river and the nature of the land were all confused. He sank ankle-deep, shin-deep, waded to where water ran deep as his waist, felt how the river could easily wash him away, how the ground could easily take him into itself.

The boy whispered:

Mister! Come back out, mister!

The lad's feet and hands dangled in the water. He leaned down and kissed the face at his breast, leaned further, held the lad on the river's surface and felt the tugging of the tide. Lowered his arms, let the lad be washed away, saw how the water held him for a time, saw the gleam of his young body heading to the piers and the sea until the water and the dark engulfed him.

Stayed there, the silt settling around his legs, imagined the lad tumbling in the river's heart, ending the journey begun so long ago.

Behind him, the boy watched. And the other children, gathered further back.

Mister! Come back out, mister!

The silt and water sucked and splashed as he freed himself. He came out clumsy and stiff on all fours and the boy crouched with his hand stretched out to help. Took the boy's hand, came to the drier firmer ground where he knelt, gathering his breath.

Who was it?

Couldn't speak, couldn't think. Profound silence in him, emptiness. He stood up and made his way back across the Middens. The children watched, they muttered together, they huddled over the trench and dipped their fingers into the black. They picked out old small coins.

Who was it? they whispered, filled with fright.

Mister! they called.

He climbed the ladder to the empty quay, stepped over the discarded rope. Clothes and skin all blackened, great splashes of black falling from him. He took himself back towards the town. Once, he would have been troubled by his state, but he knew that the day had ended now, he would soon be covered by the dark.

AN OPEN LETTER
TO MIKE BLACKBURN

Martin Stannard

Dear Mike,

All through the many weeks staring at the pile of books I carried away from your house for possible review in *Sunk Island*, there's been that unfortunate but familar feeling of having one's feet fairly well secured in the sludge that seems to cover a lot of the floor of the little room we call 'Poetry'. I've been doing quite a lot of reviewing lately, and I'm quite aware that it's possible to become sadly jaded. Most of what one sees is flat and ordinary, and it can be dispiriting. I think years of editing a poetry magazine can have the same effect, though arguably the side effects of doing that can be worse, because most of what one receives in those manilla envelopes (the same envelopes that nightmares come in) is just plain terrible. One is always having to remind oneself, with a shake of the head to clear it, that poetry is a quite remarkable art form, but an art form that a lot of people seem quite intent upon rendering inane and pathetic. But though jaded is possible, I don't think that's the case here. It's still possible for a poetry book to come along, more or less out of the blue, and make me thankful for being alive, and a part of all this - whatever it is. A couple of weeks ago, I was visiting Derek Woolf, who edits *Odyssey* from Coleridge Cottage, down in Somerset, and I came away from there with a clutch of review copies, one of which, by a Canadian called

Don Coles, is just such a book. While I was reading it, I told Miranda more than once, and in very clear terms, and always apropos of nothing that was going on in the house at the time, that it's a brilliant book- and I'm sure you'll believe me when I tell you, I don't spray such praise around very much, or unthinkingly.

It's true, unfortunately, that more often than not when I do find a book to enthuse over, it's not by a British poet. (The last book by a British poet to thrill me so much was Peter Sansom's *January*.) And because we're focussing here on British poetry, and you won't let me even mention Kenneth Koch's latest, *One Train*...

Look – British poetry is still a very tough bit of old boot leather to chew on. People talk a bit about 'bloke-ish-ness' in poetry; ignorant people seem to think it's something quite new, but that colloquial everyday tone, and things, real things we can recognise, of course goes back a long way, and in truth, there were as many crappy poems about beer and love and stuff in magazines like *Bogg* and *Sandwiches* in the late 70s as there are now. No better, no worse. Just crappy...the poetry is not going to be interesting *because* of those 'real' things. It has to be interesting before it gets to those, which means that what you have to say has to be interesting. But I suppose everything is interesting to *somebody*.

We've always known that most poetry is plain, straightforward dull. To hear people moan about poetry readings, and how few people go to them, or about the poetry audience in general, and how small it is – we've all been there, and done it, I think, but has there ever been a surprise there, really, when even at one's most generous, the best one can do is describe so much poetry as 'ordinary', or 'unremarkable'?

Then there's the poetry you're actually *meant* to admire. The kind of poetry that's by someone so bloody clever it's a wonder they don't just publish it into the air, and communicate directly with the brains of all the other brilliant aliens. I think 'look at me, admire this' is very often a sub-text to poems, and even intelligent people have the right, and probably the intelligence, to look the other way.

Anyway, I'd been staring at this pile of books, and in a moment of quiet desperation plucked out three by three women poets, just for the hell of it. I thought that 'three women' might be a sort of hook – albeit a potentially politically incorrect one – to hang something on, but I was wrong.

I don't know if Pauline Stainer, Selima Hill and Carole Satyamurti are, or aren't, three of our leading poets – perhaps they are. I don't know who sits in judgement on that kind of thing. But I'll admit I went at these books pretty well prepared not to like them, and more or less equally sure that to write about them would not feel a wholly productive thing to be doing.

This was not an unfounded prejudice. I was acquainted, if not intimately so, with the work of all three poets. I've heard Stainer read twice – on one occasion, we did a joint reading (we were an ill-matched pair, in truth, but the drunkard in the audience liked me better), and I've seen audiences either in thrall to her reading, or comatose in response. Sometimes you can't tell the difference. I know nobody was laughing, or smiling. Or showing signs of life... Whatever. I met Selima Hill once, at a bizarre event at the Totleigh Barton Arvon Foundation, when Gillian Clarke (a poet, apparently) tried unsuccessfully to get a bunch of experienced writers to play the metaphor game (another story, that) and Hill was OK, good company and all that. But her poetry, whilst it's been of some interest, has never really engaged me. And some time back, I heard her on *Woman's Hour* plugging a book, and she sounded really dull. The interviewer even managed to ask her a couple of interesting questions, but no interesting answers came back, and she sank in my estimation some-what, though I didn't care all that much. (I've become accustomed to poets on radio not saying things of great interest.) I've also met Carole Satyamurti at Arvon, when she 'guested' for my co-tutor, Michael Laskey, and myself. She wasn't my choice; I think she is a friend of Michael's. Whatever, I can't remember much about her visit, or about her. And her poems, when I've read them in magazines, have made next to no impression on me.

So what was there to say about these books that would be interesting? Are they anything at all to do with 'what's going on'? I don't know. I do know I don't like them, and I can tell you why. But I can do that pretty quickly.

Perhaps Selima Hill's *A Little Book of Meat* is not her best book. What I do know is, if you took all the similes out of it you'd have bugger all left. The book bulges with them. There's hardly a poem unburdened by them. If you're not careful they fall out all over the carpet, or if your hands are sweaty, they stick to your fingers, and when someone asks you how you are, you say that you feel like a toilet cistern that's unflushed on the borders of the new Czech Republic. Not because it makes sense, or is apt, but just because. The editors of the Bloodaxe *New Poetry* anthology would have us believe in Hill's 'centrality to the new poetry', but come on, lads: even if we accept such a thing as 'the new poetry' this is a bit much. And as for their other claim, there's really very little, if anything, that's 'anarchic' about these poems, unless anarchic poetry is untethered poetry, devoid of control because lack of control, or editorial restraint, is intrinsically good. Subject these poems to close scrutiny, and they show up as thin and unrewarding as gruel.

Carole Satyamurti's *Striking Distance* is one of those books that you need to be in a certain frame of mind to read. But I don't know for the life of me what that frame of mind is. Certainly it doesn't do to try and read it if you're feeling buoyant and bright. Each poem starts in a bag somewhere down around your ankles and hangs there determinedly. It's not that the poems are depressing, exactly. Or at least, they do not necessarily treat of the depressing. But I find it awfully hard to be interested by them, or get further than the first few lines. The poet obviously inhabits a slightly different part of this dimension than I do. That's fair enough, but I was really struggling to be patient enough or generous enough to read all this, once I'd realised that here is a poet who dares write about the disaster that occurred to the North Sea ferry *Herald of Free Enterprise* in the way Satyamurti does in 'Sister Ship'. I'm of the school that holds the opinion that unless, in this instance, you've been up to your eyes in the dark and freezing North Sea, or watched your child float face downwards in a foot of black water in your cabin, or had to bury your dead…well, I think if you've been there, and then find some poet filling half a dozen pages of their book of little poems with soft ideas the way this poet does, this is where poets and poetry can, with some justification, be told to fuck off. I think for poets like Carole Satyamurti, poetry is something actually very nice. It can treat of horrible things, but it still ends up being nice. I say this having read her book from cover to cover. There's a little poem (I say 'little' because they all feel little) almost at the end of the book about women – ordinary, unsung women – which I'd have thought was a pretty important 'subject' – but there it is, tucked away innocuously, just another little poem…Have a thought, write a little poem. What then? A gin and tonic?

Also in the *New Poetry* introduction there's some guff, in amongst the literary-critical fluff, to the effect that Pauline Stainer's poetry places her among writers who use science as subject and method. This may well be accurate, but they neglect to say how uninvolving it can be. *The Ice-Pilot Speaks* is beautifully written, and is by far the most accomplished and the most interesting of these three books, but I've not yet been able to gather up the generosity of spirit it would require of me to work my way through the title poem. And 'work' is the correct word – there's so much stuff I don't know, that the poem requires me to know… okay, make use of science and particular knowledge, but when you get on that particular poetry bus, I'm likely to wait for another one, whose passengers are just as Aruldite (a joke ©, I think, Rupert Mallin and/or Keith Dersley) but whose poems don't labour the point quite so much. There's a significant difference between the work required of a reader of, say, John Ashbery, and the work I need to do to read Pauline Stainer. I have to do it with a dictionary close at hand, for one thing. (And yes, I have to 'work' to read Pound, but strangely, it seems more worthwhile, somehow. Maybe that's another story.) I don't know. But I do know how 'fine' this writing is; it's just that I actually rather loathe it.

This is as much as I want to write about these books. Miranda made what I thought was a quite interesting remark the other day. She was browsing through these books, and some others that were kicking round my desk, and she was reading the back covers, those pompous blurbs and terrible photos of 'the bards'... and she said something to the effect that there's all this hot air on the back of the books about how this poet writes about this this this, and that poet explores issues of that that that, but there's nobody writing, apparently, because it's exciting, or fun, or because they're happy. Of course, poets who do work from that starting point, or who do have a somewhat more invigorating approach to the poem and its relation to our lives, do exist – but you have to look hard for them, and though 'happy' doesn't always come unqualified, I think a little life-enhancing poetry isn't too much to ask for, and when I'm really thinking about that, and am in the mood to *demand* that, these particular poets – are they at all representative? – are on a complete hiding to nothing.

I once wrote a very long review about some magazines emanating from a particular neck of the poetry woods – magazines like *Reality Studios* and *Rock Drill* – and poets like Allen Fisher and Anthony Barnett, I think – and gave them a fairly rigorous kicking. In response, someone accused me, in print, of being a 'bit dim'. I think it was dim, anyway. I can foresee someone chucking the same, or a similar, brickbat my way over this. But so it goes. If these books 'deserve' a more thorough scrutiny, I'm sure someone somewhere will give it them. The poetry world is full of boring people, sycophants and champions of the dull, after all.

There is a certain sensibility that can't help but resist some aesthetic postures as readily as it warms to others. Then again, a sensibility can be 'informed', and I try not to hurl criticisms around from an uninformed standpoint. But no matter how 'educated' one is, the hardest thing to learn is that it's OK to do what Frank O'Hara challenged us to do: 'go on your nerve'. But it's awfully hard to do that, though you really have to try, and believe in the fact, and remember the fact, that the nerve is a pretty well educated and informed one. So I trust in it, or try to. Years ago, when I first encountered published poets, and magazines, and all the poetry paraphernalia, there was a real sense among some of the people I was with of there being some kind of fortification that needed to be attacked, walls broken down, and people called to account. All that 'barbarians at the gates' shit. I think that's always there, somewhere, among some people, and so it should be. The remarkable thing is that now, when poetry is allegedly much brighter and more popular than it's been for, ooh, for ages; when it's on Radio One; when there's a 'new poetry' and a 'new generation' of poets, when it seems we're being told that the barbarians in British poetry have well and truly stormed the crusty city…all that – the remarkable thing is, that much of this 'new' poetry isn't actually all that different in essence, or in character, from what went before. Pauline Stainer is a New Generation Poet! It says it all really.

There are still tired recipes for poems:– Something happened to me, right? And here's a poem about it, and what it means. (OK) Or this thing happened to someone, and I thought I should write a poem about it. So I did. (Gee, thanks.) Or, I know all this wonderful stuff, and here it is: in poetry! You don't understand it? I don't care. Some people do understand it, or say they do, and I wrote it for them.

Poetry? Yeah, right. I'm going to avoid a sweeping generalisation based on these three little books, but if – if – there's a brave new world of bright new poetry out there, these are certainly not representative of it.

Of course, I don't really think there is such a world. There are loads of poets, loads and loads of poets, and as much tedium as ever; for every healthy and fresh-voiced Geoff Hattersley there's a whole clutch of Pauline Stainers, and wagon-loads of Carole Satyamurtis coming up behind... and it's usually out of this assortment of dull souls that the prize-winners and the *Kaleidoscope* features come. So what's new? Once upon a time it bothered me. I wanted people to know I was there, outside the gates of the city, with the barbarians. Now I really couldn't give a damn. Or much of one, anyway. I hate it when great stuff gets trampled in the dirt while tosh gets all the garlands, but you can't let it blight your life, or let it inform your poetry, for that matter. Poetry and its world is just like life, really, and you know what *that's* like.

> With all best wishes,
> Martin

Many improvements have been made to Main Cookers since this veteran was designed. But the fact that it continues to give satisfaction after 50 years service is further proof that the Main has always been "the best of its time". The post-war models will carry on that proud tradition.

THIRTEEN WAYS OF LOOKING AT A TURKEY

Ian Duhig

I

Talk Turkey, He told me.

II

The Sick Men of Europe; male poets are total hypochondriacs. Yeats wouldn't really have let the masked men near him with their spoons of monkey-knackers dripping like black lychees. Sweeney thinks he has died three times by heart attack. I keep a gynaecologist on my personal staff.

III

Amerika. Ben Franklin, that clever man, proposed the turkey as his new country's national bird. However, an eagle saw the Turkey off to Blighty, there to symbolize the Special Relationship. In poetry it still does, according to Amerikan reviewers of T'New Poetry. They say most of the (O so many) Brit imitators of their poets, well, suck...

IV

...And Those Fellatio Poems? Gobble-gobble.

V

Nairac's Anoraks: What percentage of Muldoon fans, like, understand what percentage of his, like, work? The key! The teeny-weeny key!

VI

Gubu Roi: Brits don't say Deutschland so why Eire ? In Northern Ireland, Unionists use it to make their southern neighbour sound distant and foreign. But the Republic – the one republic our pathetic archipelago has managed – should be given its honourable title. The turkey is involved in what you think you know.

VII

Sestina Lente: if Muldoon (as Swinburne before him) has to rhyme a sestina to make it interesting, surely that indicates something about this Provençale puzzle? Surely enough of them have been written for this and the next millenium?

VIII

Away with this serious talk, let us turkish this text into a merrier colour (Harington, 'Ulysses Upon Ajax').

IX

A good ding with firedogs sends them grovelling on to the turkeys. The turkey carpets. The Oxbridge bastards.

X

Faber and Faber Are one. Faber and Faber and Turkey-Lurkey Are one.

XI

Skies might fall an' British poets not risk their line, gurgleth Turkey-Lurkey. Are British poets total moral sick men and women of Europe, yes or no? Have you stopped beating your wife Mr. Lurkey, if you can uncork your nose from Carson's arse long enough to say yes or no?

XII

Po-mo: the word that should no longer speak its name now has the analytical value of 'groovy' and the taxonomical exactness of 'thing'. Hang it, burn it, serve it on a bed of wasms with Martian Sausages and cranberry sauce.

XIII

Small or large, *Poetry Magazine Editors* act like Somalian warlords in the deserts of poetic recognition. Feeding on the greed of poets and poetasters alike to smear themselves with print, they'll throw together any old shite that suits their murky purposes and get their local arts body to fork out for its publication costs (it should be remembered modern turkeys, like modern bulldogs, cannot reproduce without assistance). Many have unpleasant personal habits or affect a long-unfashionable devotion to failed mass-murderers (Turkey Trots) - Michael, what are you doing with that axe? Michael? Michael?

press advertisement, 1944

from PAUL KLEE'S DIARY

Peter Hughes

4

warm gusts from the funnels
dodge & turn on deck
ghosts of hope

a host of midnight lights
shows the ferry approaching
then passing by

a generation keeping to some flawed
& unacknowledged schedule

night sits out on deck
flappy wet wind pouncing on metal edges

the thick cream coats of paint
hug our gentle rust breathing its waves of pain
beneath the hopeless surfaces

fat ferry engines sound like the neighbours'
generator a few gardens away
powering the tools & components
of some unexceptional hobby

I lean over the rails
high in the saturated starless sky
& imagine Dante or someone saying
it's no good turning up the gas
if the pilot light's gone out

from PAUL KLEE'S DIARY

Peter Hughes

5

I gave you everything

storms continue to bat the country about

the cat has come home
after six months
savaged by hunting

I gave you nothing

I have the south in the pit of my stomach
in the gaps in my skull

I feel my places being taken
as dusk falls & swan fly in
from the west in loose skeins
veering left just above the water
to touch down into north-west wind

I need to be a thousand miles south

as for us
sometimes even galaxies which collide
being mainly space & silence
simply pass through each other
with just a few local clicks & flickers

HELL

Brendan Cleary

The woman with one eye thinks I am the devil. She won't leave me alone, leave me in peace with my half-finished paintings. If the phone rings in my studio I always know it will be her. She taunts me : 'You have the look of Satan about you.' She once hissed loudly down the line and although she couldn't see me I began to sweat, and I shivered and squirmed.

What lies behind her black eyepatch? I imagine there is a wide deep hole I could poke a finger into. A hole into her skull. This sort of thought would disturb my friends if they knew about it. If she really were the Devil I wouldn't be painting the glorious trees and leaves. I'd he painting naked angels.

One day I remember she brought me a cake and told me it was so sweet and delicious. When I took a bite I gaped and wretched and spat it out on the floor. It was a small taste of hell.

A long time ago I prayed. Now that she is due here at the studio any minute I try to recall all the words the priests said I should never ever forget, but my head feels blank. All I can see when I sleep is her one eye, bright and glaring, from another half-finished canvas I'll destroy. Is this normal?...

from 'Sad Movies'

CHICKEN & SEX

Brendan Cleary

Chicken & Sex. That's what I need, constantly. I am quite insistent upon this but as usual she ignores me. Sometimes, in the stillness, only the flakes of snow or leaves falling, sometimes it feels as if she is the one with all the problems and I am the Therapist. It's costing me £20 to feel so special.

What's happening now behind her eyes? I've just been revealing to her what l truely need and crave. Chicken & Sex. She just gazes at the flakes of snow or leaves falling outside in the stillness. I can hear the Police helicoptor overhead. Perhaps that is why she is so silent.

Does all this Therapy mean my entire childhood happened in some sort of warzone? Answers! I want them! Once she asked me what colour I would paint the world. That really stumped me. I made one up. A bright shocking yellow. Something that would distort all of our heads. Then she told me I masturbated too often. How could she have know that? She may be silent but she's wise.

One day when the flakes of snow or leaves weren't falling I arrived early, let myself into her studio. She had left me a virtually illegible note. I think it read: 'Gone to see my Therapist'. So she had one too! I was reassured. I noticed when she did appear she looked pale and her clothes didn't seem to fit. I know what that feels like. At that stage I had yet to mention anything at all about the Chicken & Sex. Those were happier days, less confusing. Now she tells me again over the decaffeinated coffee that I'm 'getting there'. I still don't know where she means...

from ' Sad Movies '

MOTHER

Brendan Cleary

The passageway leads down past the room with the locked door. As a child I used to pretend that inside were the sort of secrets people would plot murder to learn. Eventually Joan let me look within. She knew my father would punish her severely. He had done so before, she claimed, spanking her with a cane. But Joan could tell how much I yearned to visit this secret chamber. She died last year. My father wore dark glasses at her graveside.

In the corner there were racks of old wine bottles. Dust in the air was so thick I coughed loudly when Joan let me in. 'This is where your mother took all of her lovers' she whispered. When she said that word, 'lovers', her eyes flickered. I sensed, even at such an early age, that desire was all around me and always would be. Now that I've grown up and had experiences I still think of the expresion on Joan's face and the expression on my mother's face in the faded photograph I found on the mantelpiece. I was forbidden to mention her for many years, my father standing over me forcing me to count and spell when I wanted to run wildly through the fields.

The passageway leads to the end of all my dreams. Now Joan is dust. My father was finally discovered and all of his depravity revealed to the world. The authorities came and took him away and took away his whips and clips. I felt great relief. Now in the mornings I wake and watch the sun glinting on my mother's face in the photograph with it's dark erotic stare...

from 'Sad Movies'

37

Brendan Cleary

For years she thought he had no living room furniture. She'd never, upon 37 visits to his apartment even caught a quick glimpse of the living room's interior. It was a mystery. She would never comment upon his style or taste because she never entered. It was always, without fail, a case of his hand down her knickers in the passageway. They just didn't have the time for discussion of lampshades or coffee tables or his choice of Expressionist prints if he had any.

Ah the slow relentless passage of the seasons! 37 times, 37 orgasms on the hall mat. Rain falling on the porch used to frighten her witless. She used to imagine his other woman when it rained. There was no rational explanation. There seldom is. It scared her witless anytime, the thought of his other woman, but especially when it rained.

'One day it will have to end' she mused. They were lying in the hall, her tights askew, his boxer shorts clinging to his ankle making him look stupid. His unopened bills were scattered about. Once she had to step over a toy tractor his son had lost. She squirmed. 'One day it will have to end'

from 'Sad Movies'

NEW NEIGHBOR

Ed Miller

H E WAS JUST THE BEGINNING OF A MAN, TWELVE OR THIR-
TEEN, IN SLOUCH CLOTHES, AN OLD CHARGERS CAP TURNED
SIDEWAYS ON HIS HEAD, ENORMOUS BLACK REEBOKS ON HIS
feet. I was in the front yard, cursing my lawnmower. A typical occu-
pation this time of year.

He sauntered over. How's it going?

OK, I said, and opened my toolbox. How's it going with you?

OK.

He looked around.

You got anything I can do? Rake leaves or something.

Gosh, I said. Not really, no. Nothing right now.

Another kid rode by on a bicycle. He speeded up when he saw my
friend.

Hey bitch, let me ride your bike!

The other kid peddled harder, disappeared down the street.

What a punk, my friend said. You sure you aint got nothing I can
do?

Sorry.

Well, he said. He sat himself on a tree stump at the corner of the
yard.

This is a nice house you've got.

43

I looked at it. A three hundred dollar a month rental with bad plumbing and bad paint.

Thanks, I said. I began to work a screwdriver into the gap behind the fuel bowl.

Live here all by yourself?

I do.

Aint got no wife?

I'm not married.

Well, he said. Why don't you go to some bar and get a wife. That's what my dad does.

Yeah?

He took a sudden interest in his shoelaces. He glanced up again, briefly.

Every time my dad goes to a bar and gets drunk he comes home with a new wife. You should go to a bar and get you a wife.

I believe my girlfriend would frown on that.

Oh, he said. He looked around.

My mom and dad split up when I was little. On account my dad went to prison. He killed this dude. But then he got out last year. I'm living with him now. Me and him. Me and my dad. Right up the street in them apartments up there.

He pointed.

I knew the ones he was talking about.

One time he told me, my dad he told me, Boxer, there's no justice in this world. What do you think?

I reckon your dad tells it like it is.

Yeah, he said.

He stood, walked to the sidefence, peeked through.

You aint got no dog, do you?

No, I said.

Where you work at?

I work at a warehouse. Across town.

What time do you get off work about?

44

I don't know. About five or so.

He walked over and looked in the living room window.

You got one of them big screen TV's in there?

Oh no, I said. Just a little one. Just a little TV.

How about a VCR?

My screwdriver slipped.

Yes, I said, I've got a VCR.

How about a stereo?

You ask a lot of questions.

I was just wondering.

The kid on the bicycle rode past again and distracted my friend from his line of inquiry.

Bitch, he shouted, I'll kick your ass!

You shouldn't speak that way, I said. It's not the right thing to do. You can't make friends that way.

I don't care about nobody.

I'd think about it. A guy needs all the friends he can get. It makes life a lot easier. More fun.

I got my homeboys.

I wound the cord around the crankpulley. Gave it a jerk. The engine sputtered. Died. I began to rewind the cord again.

Well, I gotta go, he said.

He started out of the yard.

My dad's jobbing some stuff. He'll be home pretty soon. Hey, you want to buy a gun?

A gun? Whoa. I shook my head. Not right now, thanks.

My dad, my dad he gets lots of them. He sells them. Sells other stuff too. Know what kinda other stuff I mean? He put two fingers to his lips like he was taking a long pull on a Marlboro.

I get the picture, I said. I'll keep you in mind.

My friend walked off up the street, in the direction of the dilapi-dated apartments, a tangle of sorry flatroofed squalor that ranged along the far side of the old transit yard.

At night the complex has the look of Grand Central Station, new cars and rustbucket heaps throttling in and out of the parking lot, arms swinging out carwindows, green bills folded and dangling from fingertips, teenagers running back and forth, money changing hands. American Commerce. Every couple of weeks somebody gets shot or stabbed or beat up. An old story. Like much of humanity, the whole thing is a monotonous and stupid affair and no place for kids, but how do you snap your fingers and change the world?

I don't know how to do that.

A new burglar alarm went in at my house two weeks later and so did cast iron security bars all around. Three grand for the entire arrangement, including labor. A fair to middling price for peace of mind. Now I live in a fortress that would thwart even a horde of Mongols.

Of course my Doberman cries when I leave for work in the morning but I figure like me he'll get used to it.

press advertisement, 1944

WHO'S IN CHARGE HERE?

Sean O'Brien

> *Cultural change is seldom straightforward. Successive peri-*
> *ods overlap; progress is ragged; within a prevailing climate*
> *of opinion there can be innumerable variations. It takes a*
> *major social catastrophe for the main outlines of a culture to*
> *be radically transformed, and even then the old habits are*
> *liable to prove remarkably persistent.*
> JOHN GROSS
> *The Rise and Fall of the Man of Letters ('Epilogue')*

I F IT IS A FICTION TO RECALL A PREVIOUS AGE OF CULTURAL COHER-
ENCE, WHEN QUESTIONS OF LITERARY MEANING AND VALUE COULD
BE ARGUED ON MORE-OR-LESS COMMON GROUND, IN MORE-OR-
less common language, it is none the less the case that present
circumstances go some way to explain and perhaps prolong the
appeal of that imaginary consensus, for all its baggage of class and
self-interest.

The contemporary general reader (another, though necessary,
fiction), never mind the academic critic, can hardly fail to be aware
that for more than a generation the discussion of literature has been
complicated by the questions literary theory has raised about what
reading involves; about the interpretation, the definition and the
ownership of lite rature; and about how writing is to be valued, and
by whom, and for what purpose. These develoments have been one
feature, perhaps the most potent, of the attempt to revise the world
from within the academy rather than the public political sphere.

I say 'can hardly fail to be aware', and believe this to be so; yet in practice the review pages of newspapers, through which readers receive much of their sense of the contemporary, have scarcely been affected at the level of method and style. Indeed, one could argue that a rearguard action against Theory has been fought before Theory has gained much access at all to the review pages. Common Sense, dread gift of English life, has been quick in its efforts to avert such a threat.

One could also argue that even to consider Grub Street reviewing as part of the same enterprise as academic criticism is an error. Much public literary discussion continues to be carried on not by academics but by journalists and writers whose vocabularies may be barely coloured by the terms of academic criticism. They work in a context where criticism and commentary shade with worrying ease into that profiling of personalities which is the subject of Roland Barthes's essay of thirty years ago, 'Writers on Holiday'. People may be interested in books, but most of them are more interested in people: this is part of the problem, and it leads one to see something of what Lenin might have meant when he spoke about changing the electors rather than the government.

In parallel with this concern with the glamour of personality (which is of course neither new nor confined to literary matters) there is a strain in academic criticism which seeks to dismantle the hierarchy of literary worth and replace it with a frank admission that a society is allowed to want the culture it wants. It will thus be legitimate to refer to *Middlemarch* as a 'costume drama', to think *Pride And Prejudice* improved by the insertion of sex scenes, and, in the case of Professor Terence Hawkes, to find *The Bill* more appealing than Shakespeare. Indeed, Hawkes goes further; in the light of Theory, he would argue, the depth of insight and the verbal power long attributed to Shakespeare are something we, the audience, put there. To respond that this speaks highly of us, while at the same time noting that it would be hard to ascribe comparable qualities to *The Bill* at its best, is unlikely to settle the matter for the troubled phenomenologists of cultural theory, whose preoccupation with power leads them to throw the baby of value out with the bathwater of class.

The interior complexities of theory are considerable and fascinating, but to engage with them in detail may mean talking more about theory than what were once the primary objects of literary criticism – i.e. fiction, drama, poetry and other material difficult to name and thus delimit. For some this would be a legitimate activity, but for a poet interested in understanding the poetry of the times it could be one more means of marginalizing an art which, despite recent signs of public interest, has a life more proverbial than actual in the public mind.

These essays are, I hope, continually aware of the historical, social and economic forces which go to form poetry. At the same time they presuppose that in the imaginative sphere poetry has powers at its disposal which lend particular poems particular authority; they also presuppose that some poems can be shown to be better than others, i.e. more interesting, intelligent, subtle, musically alert and imaginatively startling, more attuned to past, present and future: in short, more serious, more memorable, with more to offer. These, I would suspect, are among the qualities most poets search for in the poetry they read. They are certainly qualities open to scepticism, but the imagination in action nonetheless finds them useful and durable constructions on which to rejoice. It is surely interesting that, in a period of scepticism about meaning and value, much of the best energy in writing in the British Isles goes into poetry, an activity predicated, however uneasily, on the existence of both.

In William Friedkin's recent film *Blue Chips* the basketball star Shaquille O'Neill plays a young player acquired for a college team. With the other newly-arrived players he sits unhappily in a lecture (an orotund belle-lettristic professorial performance) on *Sir Gawain And The Green Knight*. Eventually and against protocol he intervenes to ask the lecturer why the class are studying *Gawain* rather than African folktales. The lecturer replies, ' Well, because we are', and points out that the course description was available in advance. It's a funny moment in a sentimental ragbag of a film, and O'Neill's character has the viewer's sympathy. It's also a striking instance of argument about the canon making its way into a Hollywood film. The conclusion is, basically, that the professors can go to hell, because the days of deference are over. Any reader, listener or viewer will note that this is simply an economically contrived (if thematically bolted-on) instance of a commonplace phenomenon – the levelling tendency that says: my opinion is worth as much as yours because, well, because it's mine, and the inequality of my opinion would be a demonstration, not of the merits of your view in this instance, based on study and reflection, but of my personal inequality.

The opinionated condition can be seen in the sheer volume of poetry currently published. There is a well-trodden path from writers' workshop to pamphlet to first small press collection, so that an ISBN number can seem like the inevitable consequence of setting pen to paper. This would be of no interest were it not for the weird inverse relationship between the number of people who publish their poetry and the number who read that of others, which amounts to a structural reversal. To illustrate this with a sporting analogy, there are an awful lot of amateur golfers, but it would not be true to say that most of them are only interested in their own performance, since if this were so the leading players would be travelling by bus rather than private jet. Of course, the universality of language and the relative brevity of most poetry give poetry an obvious appeal as a means of self-expression, but, to introduce another comparison, the prospect of many thousands of composers clamouring for publication and performance of their symphonies would be absurd. Just as contemporary music needs an audience, what poetry needs is readers. But somebody intending to start reading poetry faces the problem of where to start, and for this reason many either don't start at all, or else treat poetry as an activity whose closing date was 1914 or earlier. It is not, of course, that the cultural resource of the many has been mysteriously mislaid or removed. The audience that poetry wants, though composed in part of the descendants of the readers of *Georgian Poetry* and Yeats's *Oxford Book of Modern Verse*, consists much more substantially of those who in other times would probably have had little access to the body of written poetry. At the same time, though, it is the case that literary authority, however disagreeable its premises, has declined to a point where the interested reader can no longer alight with confidence on the contents of an *Oxford Book*, for example. Philip Larkin's *Oxford Book of Twentieth Century Verse*, widely derided when it was published, remains an inadequate account of its period, while D.J. Enright's *Oxford Book of Contemporary Poetry* is likewise, though in different ways, disabled by its own eccentricity.

Scepticism is something these anthologies have in common, but so too is a failure to effectively represent the work which makes their chosen territories lnteresting. And if there is no fundamental reason why an *Oxford Book* should be the embodiment of authority, there persists a degree of expectation that this should be the case, even though the function of anthologies has been felt to move beyond a general and necessarily belated canonizing function towards an overt advocacy of particular kinds of work, as the recent history of notable anthologies demonstrates. *New Lines, The New Poetry*, the 1982 *Penguin Book of Contemporary British Poetry* and the more recent Bloodaxe *Poetry With An Edge* and *The New Poetry* have served a polemical purpose, albeit with varying degrees of coherence. The same holds true, in more specialized ways, of a number of other well-knon titles – the countercultural *Children* and *Grandchildren of Albion* edited by Michael Horovitz, the Paladin *New British Poets*, edited by several hands, Fleur Adcock's *Faber Book of Women Poets*, and the anthologies of poetry by women published by Bloodaxe – Jeni Couzyn's *Contemporary Women Poets*, Carol Rumens's *New Women Poets*, Linda France's *Sixty Women Poets*.

Advocacy has long been a part of anthologies, as has exclusion: Palgrave's *Golden Treasury*, for example, did much to influence the popular understanding of English poetry as primarily lyric; and we can detect in Tom Paulin's *Faber Book of Political Verse* a belated answer to the disarming, pastoralizing tendency represented by Edward Marsh's Georgian anthologies – works of late-romantic reaction which have exerted a more widespread influence on the public than the more or less contemporary Imagist anthologies.

Space forbids an exhaustive discussion of even those works listed above, but it is worth restating and adding to the sequence of significant anthologies appearing in England during the postwar period . These would be Robert Conquest's *New Lines* (1956 – a whole decade after the end of the Second World War); Alvarez's *The New Poetry*, in its 1962 and 1966 editions; *The Penguin Book of Contemporary British Poetry*, edited by Blake Morrison and Andrew Motion (1982); and, most recently, *The New Poetry*, edited by Michael Hulse, David Kennedy and David Morley (Bloodaxe, 1993).

To some degree, and necessarily imperfectly, each of these anthologies illustrates an argument. In the case of *New Lines*, common sense, reason and formal shape are offered as antidotes the excesses of the 1940s (and, at any rate by implication, of modernism). The true variety of work produced by a number of significant poets represented in *New Lines* – including Larkin, Thom Gunn, Donald Davie and Elizabeth Jennings – can be seen as evidence either of the limitations of the editorial thesis, or of the enduring strengths of sound poetic practice.

A number of poets from *New Lines* survived into Alvarez's *The New Poetry*, whose argument, while assuming formal competence and high intelligence as the first principles for the poet, demanded a greater readiness to address the horrors, both exterior and (especially, it seems) interior, of the age of Auschwitz. Foreign poetry, in the agonized persons of the Americans Lowell, Berryman, Plath and Sexton, was brandished as an example of openness and scope. The self in the confessional was the embodiment of the artistic good.

Whilst one can find a considerable variety of social background among the poets in these anthologies, matters of class and domestic politics compel little interest on the part of either the poets (in subject matter) or their editors (as components of the the anthologies' aesthetics). Literature seems to be implicitly viewed as a zone of free exchange, membership of which is conferred by skill and recognition. (By contrast, the role of class, for example, is a constant preoccupation in English novels of the 1950s and early 1960s).

Both Conquest and Alvarez include work from poets who dispute, exceed or ignore the terms of the editorial argument. The same holds true of Morrison and Motion's introduction to the 1982 *Penguin Book of Contemporary British Poetry*. If Conquest's concern was with a poetic version of empiricism, and Alvarez's with the need to match the poem to the crisis of its time (both editors being in some sense therefore prescriptive of subject matter), Motion and Morrison noted an extension 'of the imaginative franchise', that is to say, an enriched sense of what poetry could deal with, and how, and, by implication, a wider sense of who could write it. At the risk of excessive simplification, but in the interests of clarity, these developments, which M. and M., like Conquest, but unlike Alvarez, saw as confidently under way in the British context, could be thought of as threefold. Firstly, poets are exhibiting a phenomenological curiosity about the world, with marked stylistic effects – i.e. Martianism. Secondly, and to some degree consequently, the possibilities of play, fiction and narration are of increased interest to them. Thirdly, the expansion of the franchise also involves a preoccupation, usually in writers with working class backgrounds, with class, history and politics.

The result is an anthology quite as uneasy as either of its predecessors, though like them it contains work by a number of those who continue to seem the most interesting poets of the period. To make sense of their chosen evidence, Morrison and Motion would really have needed to respect the *variety within the franchise*, and to have seen this as a set of related though differing responses to historical circumstances, rather than branding the franchise with the sign of one of its contributing minorities, namely postmodernism, which now seems applicable only to the Martians and to Fenton. The editors' introduction works from Seamus Heaney and his Northern Irish peers, through Tony Harrison and Douglas Dunn, then to Craig Raine and lastly to James Fenton. It is odd how the track leads back to Oxford, and it remains difficult to feel that Raine, Reid and Fenton, interesting as they are, really punch the same weight as their Irish or 'provincial' elders, even if chronology seems to grant them the last, or at any rate, the latest word.

If this discussion appears to be maintaining an unwarranted distance from actual poems, it is inescapable that arguments about literature often have as much to do with cultural power as with the words on the page which excited us in the first place. This certainly has to be borne in mind when examining the argument and the principles of selection employed by the editors of the 1993 Bloodaxe anthology *The New Poetry*, which asks continually to be seen in opposition to its Penguin predecessor.

One of the most interesting reviews of the anthology – more a review of the introduction, really – was written by Andrew Motion in *The Observer*. From his opening sentence – 'I suppose the editors of this anthology think I'm bound to dislike it' – Motion moves deftly on to the offensive, stealing his successors' thematic thunder (saying yes, above all, to 'poetry rediscovering its role as social criticism') while damning their prose:

> *This introduction is irritating because it is boring. Instead of advocacy we get publicity department guff (they reckon their poetry is 'fresh in its attitudes, risk-taking in its address and plural in its form and voices'). We get shibboleths when we want style ('Eighties Britain grieved observers'). We get assaults on paper tigers ('The post-Romantic tradition in the British Isles has perpetuated the belief that poetry and political concerns are incomparable [sic].'*

It might be fair to say that while Motion is correct to object to the gruel of committee prose served up by the editors, at the same time his dismissal of their political observations is not quite honest. With the odd exception, British poets were slow to respond to the climate of Thatcherism, and you would in particular have to look hard among Motion's metropolitan peers for any very vigorous response to it.

Having said this, the difficulty of accurate commentary is increased by the 1993 *The New Poetry* itself, which occupies the awkward position of commending variety while needing to read it as a kind of unity. Where Morrison and Motion ran aground by identifying Irish and Scots writers as British and some working class writers as provincial, Hulse, Kennedy and Morley, with no interest in 'Britishness', include work by poets from the Irish Republic as well as Northern Ireland, from Wales, Scotland, the Caribbean and India. *The New Poetry* certainly goes a greater distance than before to represent the diverse origins of contemporary poetry in English. But the rainbow coalition which results testifies more to the poets' simple contemporaneity with each other than it can (beyond a basic level) to common preoccupations, while the formal methods on display are so various as to forbid inclusive discussion.

Matters are further complicated by the character of *The New Poetry*'s exclusions. An imaginary anthology, a *salon des refusés*, the parallel-universe remix of *The New Poetry*, could include all the poets published in Morrison and Motion, plus others born before 1940 not included in Morrison and Motion (Ken Smith, U.A. Fanthorpe, Matt Simpson, Roy Fisher, James Berry, William Scammell, John Whitworth, John Mole and Alistair Elliot were among those mentioned by reviewers), and a large number of younger poets (names again mainly drawn from reviews of *The New Poetry* whose work was also, for whatever reason, omitted – Mick Imlah, Alan Jenkins, Lachlan MacKinnon, Wendy Cope, Tony Flynn, Douglas Houston, Peter Sansom, Julie O'Callaghan, John Hughes, Michael Gorman, Maura Dooley, Andrew Greig, Mimi Khalvati, John Agard, Sarah Maguire, Linda France, Don Paterson, Graham

Mort, Oliver Reynolds, George Charlton, Mark Ford, Chris Greenhalgh, Stephen Smith, Susan Wicks, Adam Thorpe, Fiona Pitt-Kethley, Jeremy Reed, Harry Smart, Philip Gross, James Lasdun, Alison Brackenbury and Neil Powell. By this stage, of course, it's raining names, and the point of the exercise may no longer be clear – even though the list of others who could be mentioned in this context – Black and Asian writers among them – could be extended several times over. The problem is not new. Twenty years ago, Anthony Thwaite wrote his comic catalogue-poem, 'On Consulting *Contemporary Poets of the English Language*', in which he in turn harked back to the alarm of a much older figure:

> *Hamburger, Stallworthy, Dickinson, Prynne,*
> *Jeremy Hooker, Batholomew Quinn,*
> *Durrell, Gershon, Harwood, Mahon,*
> *Edmond Wright, Nathaniel Tarn,*
> *Sergeant, Snodgrass, C.K. Stead,*
> *William Shakespeare (no, he's dead),*
> *Cole and Mole and Lowell and Bly,*
> *Robert Nye and Atukwei Okai,*
> *Christopher Fry and George Mackay*
> *Brown, Wayne Brown, John Wain, K. Raine,*
> *Jenny Joseph, Jenny Couzyn,*
> *D.J. Enright, J.C. Hall,*
> *C.H. Sisson and all and all...*
> *What is it, you may ask, that Thwaite's*
> *Up to in this epic? Yeats'*
> *Remark in the Cheshire Cheese one night*
> *With poets so thick they blocked the light:*
> *'No one can tell who has talent, if any.*
> *Only one thing certain. We are too many.'*

It is a bit worrying to note that the ravages of time have so far let almost all these names survive in the critical memory. To the cultural conservative, more may simply mean worse, but while to others this may not seem self-evidently true, there remains the problem of how to get to grips with the sheer volume of work available. Anyone who has worked as a reviewer, an editor or a judge is likely to know the sinking feeling produced by the sight of the umpteenth massive batch of books from which only a bare handful can be chosen for detailed attention. Publishers with small (and not-so-small) presses well know the difficulty of getting any notice for their authors' work. The devolutionary energies of contemporary writing, with its disavowal of a single presiding Oxbridge-London centre of taste and judgment, have undoubtedly resulted in a more widespread sense of the sheer variety of work available. At the same time, though, there arises the question of what readerly competence in understanding the period might now consist of, given the varieties of English, of attitudes and approaches, which can now be encountered.

There are those who would argue that rage for order, or even unease about its absence, is the legacy of some discredited attitudes, among them Anglocentricity, centralization, the imposition of minority tastes, and possessive academic obfuscation. For others, though (and many of them are poets) the necessity of making sense persists, even if they might not want to start from here or with the equipment at their disposal. It persists because beyond the barest expression of like or dislike, beyond the acknowledgement of 'relevance' or political common cause, poetry deserves a complex response. Without this, it is, for example, legitimate to suspect that poetry's current beachhead in the attention of a wider public may be temporary. However well-intended, the status of fashion accessory is necessarily a matter of the moment, and it may require more than a long spoon to sup with the devil, if the fiend in question is no longer issuing invitations. Poetry in public is often invited, and often willing, to turn into comedy, or performance, or political succour, or moral outcry, or emotional reassurance. It can, of course, be all these things and more, but it risks losing its essential nature if it does not maintain a vigilant regard for its own interests as an art made of language. Strange times indeed, to require this statement of the obvious.

This essay forms the introduction to a book
on modern British poetry
due from Bloodaxe

press advertisement, 1943

SINGING IN THE BATH

David Lightfoot

What is written without effort is in general read without pleasure.

SAMUEL JOHNSON

S TARTING NEXT WEEK, WE NEED A NATIONAL MORATORIUM ON THE WRITING AND THE PUBLISHING OF POETRY. TOO MUCH POET-RY IS WRITTEN. MOST OF WHAT IS PUBLISHED IS DROSS. MOST OF those writing what passes for poetry in this country would satisfy their literary ambitions more usefully if they confined their activities to writing letters to the editors of newspapers rather than the editors of poetry magazines. A significant number, even of published poets, are incompetent not so much because they have cloth ears and no sense of rhythm – though there are plenty of those – but essentially because they have no feel for language, or, if they have, are incapable of showing that sensitivity in their work. Their so-called poetry is life-less, flaccid, imprecise, derivative and – worse still – boring. Worst of all it is prosaic. And in addition it is depressing.

No wonder no-one wants to read it, or risk reading more of it by buying more. Once bitten, twice shy. I have lost count of the maga-zines to which I have subscribed for one issue only. I stop subscribing, not only because, if I am honest with myself, I derive more pleasure from reading *Golf Monthly*, but because I am repeatedly disappoint-ed by what I find. I find nothing to compare with the work of past masters. And this is not a cry for a return to classical values. I wish I could find a contemporary Catullus, Juvenal, Martial, Dante, Donne,

Hopkins, Eliot or Auden. All the great poets of the past, who will still be read when our generation has been quickly forgotten, were in some way life-enhancing. They reward the effort of reading them because, in addition to admiring what they have to say, one experiences pleasure from the way they have taken the trouble to arrange words to say it.

As an editor of a new poetry magazine, *Seam*, now preparing its fourth issue, I have to report that so much of the work which my co-editor and I reject is the product of misdirected talent. Many of those who submit work to us can clearly write a reasonable English sentence. (Some find even that difficult.) Indeed their covering letters are often more competently written – and intrinsically interesting – than their poems! But prose, not poetry, is obviously their medium and most of them, I cannot help feeling, could not tell me the difference between the two. This is a saddening and baffling state of affairs about which I have pondered for some time and for which I should like to offer something by way of explanation.

An illuminating and therefore useful analogy may be made between poetry and music. Although we are taught and encouraged to listen to music, very few of us are encouraged – and quite rightly so – to compose it. This is because it is generally felt that composing music – music that anyone else would want to listen to for very long – is a difficult art, a gift granted to a few, or a skill that a few more may laboriously learn. It has been assumed for too long, however, that the writing of poetry is something that almost anyone can do. If you can talk, it seems to be felt, you can write poetry.

This is nonsense but it is considered politically incorrect to say so. Nevertheless it remains true that, even though we can all sing in the bath – usually songs composed by someone else – we do not all therefore assume that anyone else must want to listen to us. That is one of the main reasons – apart from its flattering acoustics – that we choose a private room like a bathroom to sing in. My point is that most contemporary poetry is the literary equivalent of bathtub music –

amateurish and self-indulgent.

If you do not believe me, read through almost any contemporary magazine devoted to the publishing of poetry. When did you last read a poem that 'pierced your heart like a knife' (or came close to it) as Lorca once said a good poem should? Can you recall accurately one whole line of contemporary poetry? The trouble is, however, that though most would-be singers rightly and properly keep their bath-tub music private, most would-be poets have a relentless urge to make their outpourings public. But what gives them the idea that anyone else would want to listen to them in the first place or be likely to derive any pleasure or benefit from having listened?

The answer to that question is simple: publishers, editors and educationalists give them the idea. All of these are self-evidently inter-ested parties. Have I stumbled upon a conspiracy? Probably not a conscious one but there has been a discernible trend. From the Sixties onwards too many people have earned money or esteem or misguid-ed satisfaction by encouraging incompetents to believe that the poetry they write has something important to say, mainly on the grounds that they, as individuals, have written it and that any individ-ual viewpoint is *per se* valuable and therefore worth reading. The same fatuous doctrine of egalitarian value is, of course, given to speakers in chat-shows and televised political debates. The sacred assumption is always that everyone has a valid point of view and the talent to express it. Who can forget the huge increase in the number of armchair admirals during the Falklands War who confidently pre-dicted the military catastrophe that must result from an amphibious landing on those wretched islands, or the sofa generals who prophe-sied Armageddon if Saddam Hussein's Iraq were invaded? The fact that a high proportion of lay opinion expressed about professional concerns is simply moronic should remind us that it is only informed opinion – on anything – that is of value.

But who is qualified, informed enough, to speak out about poet-ry? The first qualification, it seems to me, and perhaps the only important one, is that of having read the work of the other poets. It is a not unreasonable assumption that any dead poet's work still in print is likely to contain something of value. (It is going to be a physical and economic impossibility – thank God! – for all contemporary work to be kept in print.) When it comes to deciding what to read of contemporary poetry, you will have to be selective. On which contemporary work would you, hand on heart, recommend good friends to spend their last tenner?

This, therefore, is the best advice for writers' circles, creative writing MA courses, WEA literature classes, etc, and all editors to give to the bathtub bards: stop writing poetry for at least a year; read and re-read good poetry instead; and don't submit anything for two years. The silence that will result will be comparable to the bliss one feels when banging on the wall has made a neighbour stop singing in his bath.

press advertisement, 1944

READING MAXWELL

Tim Cumming

ONE OF THE BIG PROBLEMS ABOUT GLYN MAXWELL'S WORK IS ACTUALLY READING IT. THERE IS A GREAT DEAL OF IT TO GET THROUGH AND I WASN'T SURE IF I WANTED MAXWELL IN MY head for that long. In a five-year publishing career there have been three chunky books of poems, a collection of three verse plays (he plans to write the same number as Shakespeare), and a novel *Blue Burneau* (his prose and plays share a penchant for silly names as titles), which weighs in at something like a couple of pounds in weight. I opted to miss out on the novel and the plays.

Another big problem (with poems at least) is that much of the work is indigestible. The style hits you straight away, and though Peter Forbes, the editor of *Poetry Review*, has written that Maxwell is 'one of the few poets of recent years to have invented a style', it strikes me more for its self-consciousness and its failure to communicate what I believe Maxwell intends – that is, a maximum of possible interpretations in the shortest available space – than for its occasional synthetic successes. I'm thinking here of poems such as 'Helene & Heloise' from *Out of the Rain,* where his syntactical freedoms take on a rare physicality of feeling and perception, and where the shorthand seems to work to great effect.

Unlike Simon Armitage, with whom he shares the greatest prominence of all the 'New Generation Poets', and who had pamphlets from *Smith/Doorstop*, *The Wide Skirt* and *Slow Dancer* before his first Bloodaxe collection, Maxwell came out of thin air into the world of poetry and the *Poetry Review* at the end of the 1980s. It's interesting that there were no small press pamphlets from him, no scattered appearances to scattered applause in small magazines. His first book, *Tales of the Mayor's Son*, came out in 1990 fully formed, legs kicking, with a Joseph Brodsky endorsement stuck on the rear window, car-lot style.

This is what it says: 'Glyn Maxwell covers a greater distance in a single line than most people do in a poem. There is an extraordinary propulsion in his work, owing in part to his tendency to draw metaphor from the syntax itself. He is a poet of immense promise and unforgettable delivery.'

It sounds pretty good. I like the idea of the fast poem, the athlete of syntax, the internal jump of a really great movement of lines, the line of thought that pushes you into places you wouldn't ordinarily get to. That's what a good poem is all about, isn't it?

So the *idea* of Glyn Maxwell and what he's doing is good and worth applauding. In theory I could do business with a poet like that. But then I get to the work, and the work gets in the way. Not that it has missed out on big-league prizes. Maxwell has won a Somerset Maugham Award, and he's been shortlisted for various others – the *Mail on Sunday*, the *Sunday Times* Young Writer's, the Whitbread and for all I know, the Shortbread as well. All his books are Poetry Book Society Recommendations, and so reading all three of them over a period of months (about 350 pages of poems in half a decade) I find myself overwhelmed by the distance between the poems and what is said about them and what I can make of them, which boils down to this: they seem to stick on rather than in the mind, defying profitable reading.

Take for instance his versions of Ovid for the new book *Rest for the Wicked*; the blurb assures us that this is 'really about male ambition and overreaching'. OK. Aside from the fact that this kind of working on the scaffold of the Greeks is (to me) the last refuge of the scoundrel, much of the much-feted technique, which elsewhere is a case of drowning in detailed asides, boils down to:

Death was instantaneous.
Death is always instantaneous.
Loss was instantaneous.
Loss is always.

There are perhaps some readers who think this is profound writing, but to me it is dull, straightforward, second-hand, little more than something you might find scribbled on the back of an old envelope. Parts of the sequence make for good reading. The 'Spokesman for the sun' for instance, has a Roger Cook-style narrator side-stepping a good kicking. But the meandering whole irritates like a rash, and it's hard to see it as anything more than an exercise that should have been left in the exercise book, that it's place in Rest for the Wicked is dependent on the stature of its provenance (the Classics! the Classics!) which (it's assumed) makes mortal readers bow their heads in supplication and take whatever's coming.

Or consider the lyrics from the plays he produces in his parents' garden in Welwyn Garden City, which come in the new book (and there is a collection of lyrics in *Out of the Rain* as well).

Start where you stop
Hoist the high hoop
Day, night and crop
From a skip to a stoop
Jump through the ring,
Day and night and everything
Jump through the ring,
Priest, peasant, king,
Until all pass through
then I'll jump through too.

I guess there's a certain amount of humour in this kind of thing appearing in anything other than a vanity publication, but the laughter sticks in the throat if you think that this is a writer with a serious reputation and this, presumably, is writing taken seriously. It's a struggle to do more than scan these lyrics, to read more than halfway down a page, or to wonder what his editor thought as he or she passed on the blue pencil and sent them on to press. Wouldn't work like this devalue whatever surrounded it? This is the writing either of huge self-confidence or greater self-importance; the former is unearned, the latter is unpleasant.

But these lumped-together lyrics are the gristle rather than the meat of Maxwell's writing. The hard stuff, and there is a great deal of it, goes like this.

THE GATE TO THE WEST
In are the sweet, the welcome flavours, in
Melt the appealing, the textured soften, all
Decreasing to luck, to a tiny sugary tide
Below one blissful tongue, that licks like a whole
Cat. The mouth is empty and satisfied.

A carious molar rocks at the brink of there.
Under and either side it is riddled with pain.
Love has done this, blurt the appalled insides,
Shutting their lips on air. When they part again
it will be to binge, alone, not telling where.

Its surface is complex or careless – take your pick. As in many of the poems, the lines stutter along as if they suffer from internal blockage. There seems to be no subject or underlying preoccupation at all. There are instead tiny diversions which in the end don't seem to contribute anything but an impression of sloppiness, of a praised style exaggerated beyond its own possibilities. It's a good example of writing that just doesn't know when to stop.

What is *the textured soften*; what does Maxwell mean by *decreasing to luck*? What or where is *The brink of there* ? How do these words, phrases, lines, this poem, relate to the world, to the big world of facts, to the particular world of the senses, to the happy world of feelings and responses, to anything, in fact, that asks for involvement from a reader?

'The Gate To The West' and poems like it seem to add up to a kind of knitting-circle modernity of the most dissatisfying kind, as a prime cut of bad free verse in a rhyming straight jacket, as words struggling with words rather than words struggling with the world that gives words meaning. What we are seeing here in fact is the worst of both worlds. It's hard to feel anything but irritation, and the more you read the more there is to be pissed off about.

Much has been made of Glyn Maxwell's use of syntax as metaphor (whatever that is). The way he writes has novelty, but stripped bare it's a case of using wrong words in the wrong places, of breaking down tense, breaking down the distance between object, viewer, speaker, to a flat plane. Take this from 'Desire of the Blossom'

> *This strain bloomed red. became tended:*
> *Admirable, colourful, a flower*
> *In the good corner. No more green wildfire*
> *Threatening no promising: that*
> *Pollen-coaxing*
> *Act had ended.*
>
> *And eyes had me, noses neared and dwindled.*
> *Cameras' mutated insect heads.*
> *Partakers came to tag all sorts of reds*
> *They marked in me.*

However many times I read it, it never comes out right. It has an air about it not of urgency, as the staccato style might suggest, but of procrastination, and the internal rhymes do more to deflect attention than to carry it. Parts of the poem lose me completely and when I get back on course it's hard to know why I'm there in the first place. The impression after prolonged reading is one of leaden triviality. All his most excessive poems share this problem.

On the back of *Out of the Rain* Derek Walcott refers to 'his astonishing ability to orchestrate asides, parenthetical quips, side-of-the-mouth ruminations into a formal verse with a bravura not dared before'. And he goes on, 'His poems have the vigour and freshness of first drafts, but they are more finished and rewarding than most contemporary verse.'

As with what Brodsky says about syntax-as-metaphor, all this sounds interesting, but though you can see it happening in some of the poems, in too many of them it just doesn't work. There is a lack of drama. It is as if the curtain is coming up on something interesting, line after line, and then it comes down for good, and the poem's over.

In the end, it's hard to know how to read poems such as 'The Gate to the West' or 'Desire of the Bloom', to see how the rhyme and rhythm, the poetic special effects, create any effect at all. Each phrase, each line, follows one after the other apparently without building on what has already gone, until I find myself desperate for some kind of resolution other than the end of the page. But remember, folks, that if it doesn't all add at least you can say it rhymed. One shouldn't underestimate the importance of rhyme in the eyes of a certain kind of critical audience, because with Maxwell, I have the impression that the fact that he attempts to rhyme, however poor the result can be, the attempt itself is one of his most important attributes. It's obscure but it rhymes! This is the way forward! (A reviewer once suggested that Maxwell represented half of the future of English poetry; you can guess who the other half was. So perhaps it's time to point out here that English poetry doesn't have a future. It has, or had, a present, but even that seems debatable these days.)

Stop by the calendar, though,
And peel. The colour today
Is Yellow, and you will never remember
What that means – 'J'.

I get the sticky feeling that the sense and movement of too many of the poems are propelled by the need to rhyme, that they'll go anywhere, for anything, even split innocent words in two, to get *I'm* with *pine* to get *pain* with *gain*. It is the first time, I think, that I have encountered light verse that is difficult to read.

The way Brodsky, Walcott and others describe Maxwell's work, you would expect something fresh, hard, brittle. In fact it often seems that there is no hard core to his work, that it is all padding, writing for the sake of writing rather than writing that is doing something, saying, presenting or being something that you could recognise in your own life. Subject is sacrificed to the vaunted style, and even his most persistent supporters (P. Forbes) admit 'an extreme evasiveness of subject matter', of his work 'lacking the recognisable human moods we look for in poetry'.

An engagement with the world, even if it is the world of egg custard, is essential in any creative endeavour. I am not arguing for the tyranny of the domestic setting, or the hard detail of the external landscape or the political landscape, though since we're all in one it would make some sense. You can have Norse Gods dancing in a laundromat for all I care, and poetry doesn't have to reveal itself all at once; one piece of clothing at a time is OK. I'm not bowing down to the gods of explicit simplicity; good work has depths, shadows, secrets, a funny way of talking, but it is not an inexplicable space either. There's nothing more irritating than cleverly-articulated meaninglessness, or the commonplace paraded with a knowing smirk in outrageous costume.

In 'The Great Detectives' for instance, from *Rest for the Wicked*, one finds a half-cock catalogue of stale, half-drawn characters, It's a dull idea to begin with and just gets duller. This is rhyming Cluedo enveloped in poetic fog through which nothing is explicable. Here and in the longest Maxwell poems, 'Out of the Rain' and 'Tale of a chocolate Egg', one has the impression of someone with talent doodling, a writer stuck with nothing much to write about and a great desire to write. 'The Great Detectives' is just one of many poems without purpose, a revolving door into a building the hasn't been built, or even planned. It simply goes on and on, down one page and on to the next, given a semblance of order only by the incessant rhyming which much of the time seems to clang rather than to ring true.

> *Who hangs about that drawing room alone?*
> *None now, where failures trot to the great chair*
> *And ring around its ankles like a fair.*
> *Then everything is epilogue, is known.*
> *After the accusation's shot and stuck,*
> *Who's left will make an innocence of luck.*

I'm not asking for polemic, or for a poet's world-view to agree with mine. I'm easily attracted and distracted by obscure work that takes time to clear, that moves fast, that cuts and jumps in ways that only poems can. But a poem like this one has its back turned to the audience; as its reader I don't know where to begin. Nothing adds up and it spoils what enjoyment can be gleaned from individual images and lines and ideas. And again the sneaking feeling that *fair* is there to rhyme with *chair*, that *everything is epilogue, is known* has no meaning outside of its stitching up with *alone*.

Essentially, what's missing so often is a sense of internal logic, of anything of pressing importance forcing you to read on. Halfway through reading Maxwell's books, I got hold of Martin Stannard's collection, *A Hundred of Happiness*. He is not the world's most explicable poet either, but if Stannard writes poems that are strange, self-contained, separate entities, which work and run by their own logical jumps and cuts, and whose logic may be off-the-wall, nevertheless there is a dramatic unity to each poem that adds up to a satisfying whole. The details and asides, the surprising juxtaposition of casual phrases with surprising twists form a narrative that propels you on to the next line, the next stanza, to the end of the page and on to the next. If something that jarrs appears in one of his poems it gets used, it has a purpose, even it at first it seems inappropriate. Its internal logic makes for strong, elastic poems that keep changing when you go back to them, but they have a shape. With Maxwell, it's really hard to discern a shape, any clear purpose. The elastic is stretched beyond breaking point, beyond the point of concentration, and as a result the poems seem trivial, unworthy of the effort gone into reading them, or even the writing of them.

Indeed, I sometimes think these are the poems that are easier to write than they are to read. They lack the imaginative discipline that gives you a finished thing. What is substituted instead is stitched-up rhyme, evasion, a kind of self-satisfied linguistic tinkering. They are populated with untelling details, asides, with abstracts that are there perhaps because they were thought of at the time (the vitality of the first draft), without any thought given to manifestation, to their adult development. It makes me think of what people say about the short story: if a writer puts a gun on the wall of a character's house on page one, by the end that gun's got to go off, it's got to be used, it's got to make its presence felt. Whatever's included had got to have an effect on the whole, in one way or another, or why include it?

In the poems where there is a greater discernment and disciplining of Maxwell's tricks and tics, there is a greater success and there is something to enjoy. I'm thinking here of poems such as 'Look a Rainbow', 'The Crimson Team' or 'Helene and Heloise' or the two poems with American landscapes, 'La Brea' and 'We are off to see the Wizard'. It's obvious that no one else could have written them and they're enjoyable to read. They are more firmly placed. 'Look a Rainbow' is full of Oxford references. 'Helene & Heloise' is a recognisable word of privilege with its own expensively-cast shadows and portents. 'Tale of the Crimson Team' is funny and oddly haunting, and the rhyme pattern, significantly, is much looser here than elsewhere. When Maxwell reigns himself in and sticks to a point (or less than a dozen) he gets results. There's a story to tell, at last. Something seems to be happening. Maxwell's bantering, slightly smirking tone, which can be unpleasant in other places, seem to work well in this tale of a boozy, unbeatable, super-confidant football team getting lost on the motorway to a game that will never happen, the team song no longer sung, the number 11 nervous at the front, the driver shaking his head at the manager – perhaps it's a metaphor for poetry, for prizes, for life, for Glyn Maxwell himself. Maxwell writes a few poems about games, and they tend to work better than his gamey poems about love or suitors or blokes or gals or skinheads chucking back 'the national drink' in some unplaceable time and place. It would be good if he *did* place his landscapes and characters more solidly and steadily. I know he can do it. It is perhaps the drawback of trying to do everything at once that in the end nothing worthwhile is done.

press advertisement, 1944

THE POLITICS OF

Sean O'Brien

When I walk by your house, I spit.
That's not true. I *intend* to.
When you're at breakfast with the *Daily Mail*
Remember me, I'm here about this time,
Disabled by restraint and staring.
But I do not send the bag of excrement,
Decapitate your dog at night,
Or press you to a glass of Paraquat,
Or hang you by your bollocks from a tree,
Still less conceal the small home-made devlce
Which blows your head off, do I, prat?
I think you'll have to grant me that,
Because I haven't. But I might .
If I were you, I'd be afraid of me .

April 1992

AWOL

Sean O'Brien

The fat-fingered leaves of the chestnuts
Have lost their particular ochre.
Lying in swathes on the grass
They're reaching the unnoticeable stage
At the near edge of winter
When detail and distance are smudged.
Mourners and gravediggers stand for a moment
In yew-framed remoteness, appalled
And in love with the very idea of themselves.
Smoke travels sideways across the estates
As if this must still be the fifties
And I have absconded. Omniscient nuns
And mad parkies are waiting in huts
And expecting me hourly. But even at this point
I see we are not the whole story,
A fact which will be the true burden
Of what Sister Mary will tell me
With whispering fury whenever we meet.
Already I grasp how her keys and her rosary rattle,
How her black shoes click over the parquet
Between the main hall where I'm not
And the corridor's end where the milk-crates are stacked
By the hot-pipes and stinking already,
Where too I am not – not at school,
Not there with the wintering bulbs on the shelf
Or the poster of autumn
In which all the animals crowd to the roots

Of a single encompassing tree, and the vole
And the stoat and the badger are folded
As if in their separate drawers. Not there.
She will speak of my mother and father,
To whom I am lent, of my soul, of elaborate penance,
But part of the time she will look
At the street where the afternoon darkens,
The smoke going past at the rooftops,
The sky which has cleared to an arctic blue glamour
Behind which the stars have been steadily blazing.
Lorries and funerals pass at the junction.
The canon makes calls in the parlours
Of all his insoluble Irish, his boots
Going over the leaves with a sound like salt
As the temperature drops
And the sirens of factories bray,
Plain facts of the matter
Which do not respond, being absent themelves.

RUNAWAY

Graham Mort

Back at base we put the record straight,
scald our throats with sweet tea,
sweat out the relief of finding nothing
and tell it how it was.

How ice broke under us as we tiptoed
the path's brink of frozen mud, our torchlight
hewing that hut from the dark, our
breath dulling its padlock's frost.

How little there was inside:
a hemp rope, an oil can, the reek
of tar and diesel, spent cartridges,
newspapers, white rigging repairing
windows with its trembling yarn.

How cattle bellowed behind us, then
a fox yelped, how the farm's stub glowed
as wind sucked it and how we heard the echo
of that name they kept throwing at thc dark.

We say how we stood listening
and how the stream would not hush
itself across the earth's curve;
how a pheasant crackled from the woods
and the sky cleared as we squinted

for satellites, bringing the Pleiades
from their fading-trick of light.

In the morning they'll let dogs sniff
at her clothes then track her.

They'll find her huddled in that nook
of larches, still breathing, dribbling
a miracle of ice from the thumb in her mouth,
only an hour from the big sleep.

Or she'll be covered with a sheet
where the flashlight sprawled her,
the forensic squad on their hands and knees
prising clues from leafmould and fingernails.

Right now we're in the pick-up driving home,
empty-handed, sleepless, thinking of bleak
headlines and black waters, of a figure
who might still drag herself from the trees
towards her father's litany of all
she had to stay for.

Needles jab and flicker on the dials,
measuring each stammer of wheels on a track
where headlights stun the sheep, bounce
from night's meniscus of sky, then
find the road and sweep it clean.

CUSTODY

Peter Tatlin

Gone, gone.

The Gaffer gone.
Buster Broker broken and gone.
L.B. lost to boys and the bottle –
Scandal, self-hatred and time took their toll.
Matron married and matronly – to schoolboys gone, good as
    gone.
The Major murdering somewhere no doubt, but elsewhere,
    elsewhere gone.
Eric Stokes – the last thing he did, Eric Slumbers would have
    been better –
Slumbers deeper now.

Boys gone. Empty halls, empty classrooms, empty dorms.
Grounds ringing with their cries, cries' owners gone.
D.J. gone to the dogs, the needle,
Others to City, to Law, to sod.

Gone great crested newts.
Gone waterboatmen, whirligigs, dragonflies, damsel and may.
Gone the oak cricket, gone click beetles and rescued rooks,
Gone their very nettles, elms and oaks.

Gone the shivering shoals of elvers ribboning up the stream.

All gone. All with me now.

THE WRACK LINE

Robert Edric

Thursday, 4th June

LYLE WAS RETURNED TO US TODAY. THOSE OF US WHO STILL CARE FOR HIM – GOD KNOWS WE ARE FEW ENOUGH – HAVE BEEN TO SEE HIM. HIS EYES ARE VACANT. HE SPEAKS TO NO ONE. Abbot says the stories we have heard are true, and we left in silence, none of us knowing what to say. I believe we were all relieved to come away, each of us fearing some small disclosure. There but for the grace of God, said Rose. Few of the tales are repeatable. There is no clear boundary here between rumour, opinion, fact and speculation: an amalgam exists that a man who cares for the truth must break with a hammer. Jameson says they will hang him for sure.

They are past caring back at Headquarters. Past caring that we here have all become the cheating and unscrupulous instruments of their rapacious, pitiful and never-ending folly.

It rained all afternoon. The compound is flooded. There is not one of our dwellings that does not now let in the water. I played cards with Jameson and the quartermasters.

Who on earth, who back out there in the world would believe what we endure? Flabby, weak-eyed devils, all of us.

Saturday, 6th June

I returned alone today to see him. His feet have been manacled, his hands tied. He cannot stand. Is it true? I asked him. I neither expected nor received an answer.

I remember what he told me long ago, upon my own arrival here: never believe a man who tells you no price can be put on human suffering. It was Lyle who guided me round the Station and introduced me to the others. It was he who took me into the labyrinth and showed me those other lost souls there groping their way out. That same night he revealed to me his collections. I remember I did not sleep, deafened by the jungle.

I thought for a moment that he looked up at me. I hoped he might trust me above the others. But there was still no recognition in his eyes. He slavered and caught the saliva in his palm to rub awkwardly into what remained of his hair. I can only imagine what he must have endured during that lost month.

On my way back to the stores, Jameson arrived with news of fresh corpses washed downriver. The sandbank where these are caught – whole, in pieces, newly dead and rotted – we call Corpse Island. Our collective imagination is corroded. It is beyond the bend in the river. Small mercies.

Sunday, 7th June

Long discussions and endless speculation. A month will pass before Lyle can be taken down to the coast.

A poorly-timed explosion in the quarry has held up work for three days. Some track is destroyed and ten men injured, six seriously. None of ours. Rose spends all morning deciding how best to disguise the loss in his ledgers.

For an hour he and I watched a man carry water from the river to his crops. He has found an old pail and so refuses to use his hollow gourds. He walks fifty yards from the river to his plot. The pail leaks, and after each journey he throws out a cupful of water to add to his irrigation. Those working on neighbouring plots are jealous of his find.

It is the small things to which one clings. Sanity and desire are winds. The injuries of ten men are nothing beside our curls of hair and milk teeth. Abbot declares that he would kill the worker who even so much as looked at the photograph of his fiancée. She has not written for ten months. He alone stakes his belief in her devotion and patience.

A false whistle sounded at noon and for an hour we stood and waited for the steamer which never came. A trick of the canopy, Jameson said.

In the evening we discussed what was to be done with Lyle's belongings, but came to no decision. There is no family.

No worship.

Tuesday, 9th June

It is said that Lyle killed a man and then in his madness severed his head to keep as a trophy. It hardly matters who believes and who does not believe this.

Upon seeing me for the first time, Lyle remarked on my hair and my clothes and said that I reminded him of a hairdresser's dummy.

I have been redrawing our maps. The territories over which our workers now roam are immense. A warning has come from Gran' Bassam of unscrupulous traders trying to sell antique ivory they have disinterred. The tributary fingers grow longer each year. There was once a plan of a railway. I cannot believe there is such order in the world. A man might cocoon himself in these charts and say they were his comfortable life.

Collections of insects and flora, of cured skins, geological specimens, bark, dried fishes, semi-precious stones, totems, river shells, weaponry, ceremonial wear, butterflies and moths. Even phials of sand in which a fleck of gold might be seen and then lost. Tales and fetishes.

Friday, 12th June

Witnesses are being sought to testify against Lyle. Few will come forward. Their fathers were slaves. Humanity and justice are grave and fill to these people. Rewards have been offered.

Lyle, said Abbot, has become a scapegoat. He says the world is changing, and that we will never afterwards possess the courage to talk of what we once were, of the lives we once led, of the riches we once generated.

Curiously, I dreamed of Lyle in the afternoon and woke only at the onset of the rain. The small apes have again taken up residence in the roof of the veranda. Rose shoots his and throws out the corpses.

Jameson believes that there are other, hidden collections in Lyle's hut. He wants to destroy them – to destroy everything – before those seeking their evidence bend aside the leaves and peer in at us.

In the night there was a great thrashing and bellowing in the river, but nothing to see at dawn. I fear a return of the sickness. There is a lake not twelve miles distant that is home to a monster.

Saturday, 13th June

Lyle has bitten his lips until they bleed. Someone has tried to apply iodine to them and left him looking like a clown. Like a child in a blackberry patch, Jameson said coldly.

By coincidence, later in the day a small quantity of indigo arrived. The trader would not accept our price – so the old trick: keep him until nightfall an then tell him to go elsewhere, that he cannot moor his vessel to our posts. I saw him later, stupefied with drink in the bottom of his boat. And because he had come, so others followed him. Some wanted to see Lyle, but were driven away. One man defecated outside his door, his mess alive with worms.

True civilization, announced Abbot at dinner, depends upon good drainage. Here we have none. In a ravine beyond the quarry lie scattered ten thousand clay pipes, every single one of them broken.

The ruins of our civilization. Like the empty holes of our buried treasures.

Monday, 15th June

News today of an overland expedition en route to one of the Inner Stations. They will be with us in three days. Again we must turn our clean and smiling faces to the world.

I visited Lyle, but still he does not respond. Efforts continue to be made to uncover witnesses.

Abbot calls it all politicking. A distant signature to a piece of paper and we will all be recalled. None of us has his fortune yet.

Lyle has been given a cup and a bowl, both hewn from wood. His boots have been taken from him, or stolen, and the iron rings chafe his shins. He seems neither to notice nor to care.

A good delivery of ivory. Jameson and the others are sorting it now. The quarry is back in operation. There is talk of rebuilding the old jetty and of the construction of a coaling station here. Rose says to ignore it, that it will come to nothing.

I recall my first view of the quarry, from the hillside above. I believed half the workers there to be already dead. Most were shackled in teams and worked to the pace of the sickest or the slowest man. We were snails riding upon the back of a tortoise. I saw the pearly joint of a living man's skeleton where it pierced his skin.

Thursday, 18th June

I took a new ledger from my tin trunk to find it half eaten by ants. Their mulch of corpses filled the base. I was overcome with rage and wept at the discovery. I see how much else I might just as easily and carelessly lose.

Thirty canoes passed us by going downriver. We hailed them, but no response. They were not people I recognised. Men had their faces white to resemble skulls. Some women urinated in the river directly opposite us. Rose stood with his Martini-Henry on them for as long as it took them to pass.

There is talk of flooding at Bassam, and of a mudslide upriver at Petit Coeur. It was unsettling to watch the canoes pass without acknowledgment. A fire burned in one of the larger craft, the first time I have seen this.

The small, one-eyed boy who sometimes acts as our messenger was with us when they passed. When they came close he scooped up handfuls of earth and buried his face in the ground. He is our bird of ill-omen.

Sunday, 21st June

A party of militiamen are late returning. They should have been back by nightfall yesterday, but had still not returned by dawn. No one can be spared to go in search of them. Whistles are blown hourly at the quarry.

Eleven men presented themselves for hire this morning. Abbot examined their eyes and their teeth and told them all they were dead men. One said he carried a diamond as big as an egg in his stomach. None of the others confirmed this. He said it had been there a month. Then it will kill you, Abbot told him. He told the others to return with the man's unopened corpse.

I waited at the edge of the clearing for news of the militia. As ever, the silent wilderness surrounding our empty speck and laundered flag strikes me as something permanent and invincible, like evil or truth, waiting only for our departure.

Monday, 22nd June

The overland expedition arrived today, four days late. We had hoped to keep the news of Lyle from them, but they had already heard. The leader of the expedition said they came to us via our quarry. He asked me if I knew what happened there, how the men were treated. I stopped myself from laughing in his face.

Later, when I was alone with Jameson, he said I should have told the man to get back to the brothels of Port Elys. He cleaned his hunting pistols. He says Lyle will not survive any journey home to put him on trial.

He gave me a book about Napoleon's battles in Egypt. He pointed to a corner of the room and said, The Nile. The pistols belonged to his father. When fired, both pulled sharply right and up a little. He uses them to create a spectacle of the roosting birds.

The pages of the book were wrinkled with damp and blemished with unstoppable mould.

Wednesday, 24th June

A witness has arrived to Lyle's crime. He saw Lyle make love to a small girl of his tribe and then afterwards kill her, cut off her hand and then cut out her tongue. He says he saw all this. He brings with him the child's other hand. He will not answer what relation he is to this child. He sits outside and constantly redraws her in the dust.

Others are more anxious to listen to what he has to say. He was not allowed to see Lyle so that he might afterwards describe him to a court. Abbot says the man is a liar.

Later, a boat passed us in which two men carried a trussed giraffe. We seldom see them so far from their usual territory. Rose says the creature will die, because once off its feet it will be unable to stand again and its heart will give out as it makes the effort to do so.

Thursday, 25th June

It worries the men of the expedition not to be able to see the coast at their backs. There is a high exposed boulder ten miles inland which is said to be the last place the cooling breezes can be felt. Once more we have been lectured on the condition and treatment of our workers.

It is satisfying to hear again the distant early morning explosions which crumble and drop the rock face.

Jameson killed a pig which arrived at the river to drink, and when he started to butcher it the animal came miraculously back to life and leapt down from the table with its innards exposed. It lived like this for a further hour.

The expedition members will touch no food other than that which they carry with them. Each day of waiting more of their porters abandon them.

A boat passes by with its limp yellow flags. Washerwomen run from the river.

No rain today.

A still and earthy atmosphere as of an overheated catacomb. What a merry dance of trade and death goes on hereabouts.

Nightmares. Weary at dawn, as though after a long journey or struggle.

Tuesday, 30th June

Lyle now stands accused of cannibalism. Another finger has been pointed. Almost a month has passed. He broods at our centre like some barely-containable, contagious and fatal disease. We visit him less and less. Abbot says he is rotting where he sits.

Today's rain flooded the landing stage. Whole trunks and tangles of foliage are swept past us in the swollen river. Small animals ride these to the rapids and provide target practice for Jameson and Rose.

A caravan. Babble of voices, impromptu sales and exchanges. Four men and two young girls in a covered cage being taken to the colony outside Ososo. Only Abbot lifts the skins and looks inside. Others turn away their heads and close their eyes.

Thursday, 2nd July

The expedition leaves us today and continues upriver. They despise us – a midden along their own shining path to glory – and want to be clear of us. They complain of the vapour-ridden air. Not one of them has been to the parts for which they are now headed. Those who survive to return to the sea will tell their tales of us.

Lyle is raging like a wounded animal. Abbot says one foot is almost severed and ought to be amputated. Sulphur powder lays scattered around his den. His uneaten food is picked clean.

His only company now is the small, one-eyed boy, who squats outside his door and plays with the pebbles which he endlessly casts across the boards of the narrow corridor.

Saturday, 4th July

It cannot go on, says Jameson. We all agree.

In the afternoon there was a partial eclipse of the sun, a crescent of black, a paring of the unimaginable.

There was no work at the quarry as a consequence. Jameson has spoken to no one for the remainder of the day. There is talk of some upheaval on the coast, new town governments, new legislation.

Sunday, 5th July

A gunshot in the depth of the night. Lanterns were lit. Some commotion and Lyle was found shot dead in his cell. A pistol pushed through the bars of his door. The powder burns on his forehead suggest that he must have manoeuvred himself to squat close to the barrel so that whoever held the gun would not waste this single merciful opportunity. Abbot has experimented. Nine inches. God rest him, Jameson said. He insisted that the body be untied and unshackled and covered with a sheet. The back of Lyle's head was gummed to the floor, his eyes shut. Praying, Rose said.

We worshipped together for the first time in a month.

Monday, 6th July

Arrangements have been made for the burial. The Company will not like it, but there are no alternatives. It will be a private ceremony, at night. The grave will not be marked, and in six months it will be lost forever. Fitting that Lyle should be swallowed up in this way. It is not his shame we bury. We here do not shroud him in our disgust.

Jameson says that a war is coming in Europe. None of us know that place.

Here, too, there is unrest, averted glances, old hatreds being burnished to a point.

None of us have worked today.

There will be no Company inquiry. No one will come. Men are made here out of nothing and men disappear into nothing.

Late in the evening, the small, one-eyed boy ran terrified into the compound, stood screaming for an hour, and then fell mute. Our questions terrified him even more, and afterwards we took it in turns to beat him until he screamed again and told us of what he had seen.

press advertisement, 1943

BECAUSE I COULDN'T SING

Peter Finch

I STARTED WRITING POETRY BECAUSE I COULDN'T SING. THE IDEA OF MAKING MUSIC SEEMED SO IMPORTANT. IT TOOK WHAT WAS INSIDE AND PUSHED IT OUT WHERE EVERYONE COULD SEE. IT COULD excite, invigorate and move people. The song and its instrumental accompaniment, especially that of the acoustic-guitar-led singer-songwriter tradition with its bardic, troubadour overtones seemed to be all there was worth having in the world. With guitar, harmonica harness and bottle-caps on the shoes I tried this and failed miserably. Even the drunks at the Greyhound scrumpy pub would not put up with my strained chords and fumbled mumblings. I gave up.

In its place I found poetry. An arena of songs without guitars, without voices, without audiences, without singers. A place where anything could happen and the rules bent about like reeds. Not quite anarchy but freedom with purpose. Formless form. Challenge and music. Excitement and brevity. Mysticism and modernism. Electricity and lying down. I wrote a few blues lyrics and sent them to Willie Dixon. Nobody wrote these things down, I discovered later. You made them up as you went. Willie Dixon didn't bother to send mine back. But I had begun on the road. There was no turning. I met sound poet Bob Cobbing, Welsh bard Rhydwen Williams, and American expat beat renegade George Dowden. Poetry was such a broad church I wondered how it was roofed at all.

And that turned out to be the secret of poetry's vitality. Its sheer breadth of style and sound and content. No one ever completely agrees over what it is and what it contains. If you don't like what you find you can always turn about and discover something equally valid elsewhere. The arguments over what exactly verse is serve to push the whole thing along. So you hate the New Gen and everything it stands for. This close, exclusive group of unvoted for nominees of the commercial publishers cannot be all that British poetry is? Turn about and check Iain Sinclair, Chris Torrance, Barry MacSweeney and the controversy surrounding Andrew Duncan's *Angel Exhaust* magazine. You'll get a view of poetry so different you'll think you've landed on Mars.

Where does poetry fit into the great UK scheme of things, asks Mike Blackburn. By and large I guess it does not. On a popular level the dub poets and the performance writers pull good, young audiences. Allen Ginsberg on a recent visit to Swansea Year of Literature had a full 800 house with so many turning away that he read again in a nearby pub just to satisfy demand. But don't be fooled. For all its London Underground zippyness and its BBC2 tv brilliance poetry is still largely a subterranean, ignored, misunderstood, freakish and financially incompetent art. If it vanished overnight virtually no one but the UK poets themselves would notice. Liverpool star Brian Patten is still on the circuit. There are more than 300 little mags in the UK. Poetry is on the Internet. Wendy Cope sells more than 60,000 copies of her titles and gets into the paperbacks top ten. How many houses in the UK have television? Virtually all. How many have books, other than dictionaries and old copies of the Bible? Not many. And on this scale how many have even one poetry anthology? Pretty near none.

What dreams do I have? I need to keep going. It has been at least twenty five years now and the muse still visits. I know how to work it. I can always write something. But the rich seams are never predictable. For the future I need more. It has become a kind of obsession. A blanket need to keep on. It no longer matters how many others are the same field and the old rivalries have largely fallen by the wayside. There do appear to be more poets working the UK circuits at present. Next year there will be fewer. The business moves in cycles around me. I plough on.

So much of contemporary poetry does little for me. I guess it was always this way. We have so much sheer choice before us. Everything cannot possibly be of worth. Among the teeming billions on this planet only a few are capable of genuine, long-term, worthwhile creation. We can all write, sure. But what we turn out is hardly ever worth a second glance. Working the Oriel Bookshop with its vast and comprehensive twentieth century poetry section, as I have done for decades, has made it easier for me than for others to prowl poetry's byways, to seek out the odd and the new, to discover what I need. Such excess makes you blind to much of the dross that appears in print. Your tolerance to crap falls through the floor.

It seems to me that much U K writing is insular, little Englandish, sticking to the white, middle-class language, the language that once dominated the world but no longer does. The real excitement can be found where that language has migrated. America mainly, where English is reworked, reinvented. Already 20% of the English used in the States is different from our own and the gap is growing. Paul Hoover's *Postmodern American Poetry* (Norton 1994) is the best collection in ten years and outruns anything we have produced this side of the Atlantic. America exploits its differences, is unashamed and runs with power and energy. We sit about apologising for ourselves and making sure our minorities get a fair crack. We fail badly. How many Welsh voices, for example, have you heard? Be honest. The answer is bound to be none.

Whatever else I do my interest is in the core of language. Words. Meanings. Their shapes. Their sounds. I'm keeping on.

transitions

*a new twice-yearly anthology
of poetry and prose
from the European borderlands*

prose, poetry, drama,
literary non-fiction

issue one includes writing by:
Gösta Ågren
Péter Esterházy
Jaan Kaplinski
Igor Klikovac
Leena Krohn
Ivan Lalić
Viivi Luik
Bronisław Maj
Karel Matěj Čapek-Chod
Dušan Mitana
Dubravka Ugrešić

out in July at £6.95
(£7.50 incl. p&p)

please write for further details
to **transitions**, 19 Queen Court,
Queen Square,
London WC1N 3BB, UK

SOFT BACK: HARD SELL

Jonathan Davidson

> *The publication of* A Handful of Stones,——'s *first collec-*
> *tion, marks the debut of a remarkable writing talent.*
> *Already one of our foremost younger writers,——has*
> *shown himself to be a poet capable of a complex relation-*
> *ship with his chosen form. In this unashamedly concise*
> *volume he gives substance to his reputation as an emerging*
> *contemporary poet, at ease amongst the detritus of recent*
> *history. He has been described by——writing in the ——*
> Review, *as 'surely one of our most exciting new poets'.*

BUY THIS BOOK? I'D SOONER DIE IN A DITCH. AND I MAY. WHAT THE BOOK IS LIKE I DON'T KNOW, BUT IF THIS BACK COVER BLURB IS ANYTHING TO GO BY IT MAY WELL BE FIRST-RATE DRIVEL from start to finish. Of course, you know that I've made this up, don't you? But every phrase rings strangely true to my ear. A few clues give the plot away. That the poet is *already one of our foremost younger writers* has one reaching for the revolver. Jealousy, yes of course. But a certain healthy scepticism as well. Notice, also, that he or she has a *remarkable writing talent*, as opposed to an uncanny aptitude for horticulture or cookery. And finally, and this is surely the back-cover kiss of death, the writer is *one of our most exciting new poets*. It's almost code for *I am destined to bore you all to death or never be heard of again.*

And if there are so many exciting poets knocking around then tell me why the nation is not gripped by an iambic frenzy? Why are the streets not lined by beer guzzling louts awaiting the open-topped bus carrying the winning *United Exciting Poets F. C.* along the primrose path to the Town Hall and Freedom of the Borough? Why? Because in nine times out of ten it just is not true. These are, as most writers will inevitably be, just regular folk, writers of good work doubtless, but not of *exceptional* talent and certainly not *one of our most exciting.*

Here are some real life examples (although I use the phrase reservedly!):

> ...*marked the emergence of an exciting new talent in contemporay poetry...unashamedly bulky collection...*
>
> ...*we see the energies of narrative and image combining to produce a poetry of complexity, yet with greater ease and direction than in some of his previous books...*
>
> *He has a voice and consciousness all of his own...both original and gripping...*
>
> ...*two of the most exciting writers in the country.*
>
> ...*full of freshness and vitality born of acute observation and yet at the same time gently nostalgic... they are never dull.*
>
> *Though he is only 28 years old, he has a fully achieved poetic voice and we are confident that this marks the debut of an important and original writer.*
>
> ...*is a volume capable, as few first books are, of disconcerting the reader.*

Ten years ago when I first became interested in contemporary poetry there seemed to be a new mood afoot. Perhaps it was my imagination but there seemed to be a desire to make contemporary poetry accessible and exciting. This manifested itself in better design, better distribution, better promotion of poetry – and of course a new enthusiasm for selling with a few well-chosen phrases on the back cover. It was clearly a reaction against the two schools of blurb writing that had previously held sway, each locked in futile combat against the other.

The first considered it sufficient to list the poet's year of birth, place of residence and to state where they were educated. And when I say educated I do not mean, as in my case, *Manor Road Infant School, Stephen Freeman Junior School* and *St Birinus Comprehensive School*. I mean, of course the *university* to which the poet went up to or came down from or whatever it is you do in those places. The assumption was that anyone audacious enough to find this kind of blurb appetising would probably be sufficiently well briefed not to require any details regarding the style or tone of the poetry. These books one did not rush out to buy.

The second school of blurb writing was equally as successful at not actually describing the contents of the book. It extolled the writer's position within such and such a movement or described the work in phrases of such inexactness and pomposity that any flame of an inclination to read the book was quickly extinguished. These books, also, one did not rush out to buy.

Neil Astley has made a similar identification of these styles in the introduction to *Poetry with an Edge*, Bloodaxe's excellent anthology. And indeed Bloodaxe broke the mould by letting a few crisp phrases and a well-chosen – and comprehensible – quote from a reviewer sell their books. Other publishers followed suit. Some got it right. Some didn't. But the idea that a book of poetry deserved proficient advertising copy and packaging became a popular one.

Now I am going to tell you that this has all changed. Well, it hasn't all changed but as my examples above illustrate – and these are all of the last few years – the ludicrous hyperbole coupled with the meaningless phrase is once more in vogue. And (and this is perhaps more disturbing) once more poets are being described as having been educated at *university* x or y as if this should tell us all we need to know – given that we are of course *in the know*.

Ten years ago I felt that all poetry was there for the enjoying. Now

I get that unnerving feeling that some is not for me or for my friends or even for any intelligent reader. I feel that far from inviting me as a reader to enjoy poetry I am expected to arrive either fully equipped with the sophisticated critical apparatus presumably available to those who write and edit poetry *seriously* or to suspend all disbelief and simply gasp in awe as poem after poem hits the high note. Indeed the notes are getting so high that only the dogs are howling for more.

I set before you a lukewarm, badly-argued conspiracy theory. The cold war is back on. All leave is cancelled.

THAT OLD DUSTER — use it to a **RAG** then pop it in the **BAG**

THAT old Duster or any other Rags or Garments worn beyond repair should go into the making of equipment for the Navy, Army or the R.A.F. Never since the war started has Salvage been more important than it is today. Worn-out clothes and handkerchiefs, old white linen or cotton collars, threadbare mats — anything you cannot use, your country needs — NOW! Put your rags — yes, even grimy ones — in a separate bundle for collection or sell them to the Rag and Bone man.

Put out RAGS — WASTE PAPER — BONES — ready for the Salvage Collector when he calls.

Never, NEVER put your Salvage in the dustbin!

Issued by The Ministry of Supply

RS.3—817

press advertisement, 1944

'OH FUCK ALL THIS LYING!'
Some Notes on the Poems of B.S. Johnson

Jonathan Coe

IF B.S. JOHNSON'S NOVELS ARE ALL BUT FORGOTTEN IN THIS COUN-
TRY NOW (AS OPPOSED TO GERMANY, SAY, WHERE EVERY SINGLE
ONE IS STILL IN PRINT), WHERE DOES THAT LEAVE HIS POETRY? TRI-
gram's paperback edition of *Poems Two* has not been available for
years. The original *Poems* is now a rare collectors' item. Every so
often these days Johnson's name will surface as part of an ongoing
debate about the experimental tradition – or lack of it – in British fiction; mention will be made of his bizarre, fundamentalist belief in
literal truth as the bedrock of all good writing, his conviction that
'telling stories is telling lies'. But what we never hear is any discussion
of Johnson's idiosyncratic concept of 'truth' as it applies to his poetic
practice. What follows is no more, at this stage, than an attempt to
raise this subject.

Poetry written by novelists is frequently treated as a mere
adjunct, and read not on its own account but for the light it suppos-
edly sheds on their fiction. We scour novelists' poems on the look-out
for clues, searching for more direct, more confessional statements of
themes we have already identified in the main body of work. In B.S.
Johnson's case, this approach won't wash, simply because his poetry
could not possibly contain anything more direct or confessional than

what we already find in the novels themselves. In terms of content, there's no substantive difference between his prose and his poetry: they are both, if we are to believe Johnson's own statements on the matter, part of the same attempt to record personal experience in as raw, honest and accurate a form as possible. The themes of his poems, then, are the same ones we associate with his most intensely autobiographical novels, *Trawl* and *The Unfortunates*: betrayal (particularly sexual infidelity) and the randomness of misfortune (particularly as it affects the body in the form of disease). Here, for instance, is Johnson going ironically against the grain of his dislike for invention, and extolling the virtues of fictional women over real ones:

> *Kim, composite of all my loves,*
> *less real than most, more real than all;*
> *of my making, all the good and*
> *some of the bad, Yet of yourself;*
> *sole, unique, strong, alone,*
> *whole, independent one: yet mine*
> *in that you cannot be unfaithful.*

'For a Girl in a Book', *Poems*

And here he is returning to the theme of disease which will haunt his writing from *The Unfortunates* onwards:

> *Urinating in a urinal*
> *I try at first directly*
> *to jet down a fruitfly*
> *then see random sprinkling*
> *is the proper method –*
>
> *you cannot beat the random element*
>
> *as in cancer, as my mother knew*

'Where is the Sprinkler Stop Valve?', *Poems Two*

Two questions are raised by these examples, one about content, and one about form. The first leads us into the area of biography, and can only be answered sketchily here: namely why, in giving expression to aspects of his own personal 'truth', did Johnson return so obsessively to the theme of betrayal? Trawling through the scanty biographical evidence which is in the public domain (most of it consisting of the novels and poems themselves) we find repeated references to two experiences which seem to have stamped themselves indelibly onto Johnson's creative personality: being separated from his parents during the war, and being 'betrayed' (or at least ditched) by a girlfriend some time in the early 1960s. Of evacuation, he wrote:

> *When I was six, the problem was to find*
> *a place for the evacuated boy,*
> *out of London danger; they stayed behind,*
> *said Grit. son! and bought me another toy.*
> *Doing the best thing for me, to their mind:*
> *war or parents: which did more to destroy?*

from 'Clay', *Poems*

And in the same volume, we find the extraordinary 'Sonnet', dedicated to Zulfikar Ghose, which after twelve lines' fulsome celebration of friendship (a friendship, we are told, that 'excludes all falseness'), concludes with the chilling couplet:

> *but when tonight you spoke my dead love's name*
> *a hatred for you spat like a welding flame.*

This element of absolutism in Johnson's personality has been remarked upon by many of the people who knew him. 'He had a tendency to take things to extremes, to take truth-telling too literally,' wrote Eva Figes: 'Bryan was a purist, almost a puritan.' Zulfikar Ghose wrote a long essay about Johnson for *The Review of*

Contemporary Fiction (Vol V, No 2) in which he went even further, maintaining that, 'Bryan carried an enormous quantity of sadness within him. Life had betrayed him, and he was constantly on the guard against fresh betrayals, suspicious of anyone who could not love him wholly ... Bryan's demand for unquestioning devotion was a measure of his love. And this, too, was perhaps a consequence of his experience with the woman who had jilted him: he had loved her with such total commitment that her betrayal was a treacherous act against his will, and, therefore, whoever loved him after her must never perform the slightest act that appeared to be at variance with his will.

This emotional absolutism seems to have spilt over into Johnson's literary politics, too. His famously combative introduction to *Aren't You Rather Young to be Writing Your Memoirs?*, which impressed me enormously when I was younger, in fact presents a series of contradictions beneath its brook-no-argument tone: one of them being that Johnson has seemingly no hesitation in consigning the entire history of the Western novel to the dustbin on the basis that 'telling stories is telling lies', yet retains his admiration for Sterne and Joyce ('the Einstein of the novel'), both of whom told stories rather than dealing in fact. Ghose, again, has an interesting take on the subject:

> *the polemical, belligerent tone of that piece, the posture of deliberately provoking offence and the suggestion that the writer is in exclusive possession of the truth and the reader contemptibly stupid if he does not accept that truth echo the way he used to argue. The voice rising, getting more irritated and excited. There was something of the bully in him.*

Although less notorious than this introduction, the 'Note on Metre' which concludes *Poems* provides a distant foretaste of its hectoring tone. Here, Johnson is defending his decision to write poetry in syllabics. 'It is as legitimate to use syllables as the element from which to form metrical units as it is to use elements like stress or quantity,' he writes, as if people had been queueing up to ban the practice. Again, we see him engaged in a wholesale writing-off of literary history: 'Since most poetry reaches its audience in printed form, a metre which is easily apprehended visually, as any syllabic one is, would seem to be more appropriate than those metres which depend upon sound, like stress or quantitative ones.' (Hard luck, then, to Donne, Milton, Pope, Wordsworth et al, who simply never saw what it was all about. But don't we, in any case, 'hear' poetry in our heads while reading it on the page?) And finally, there is the insistence that Johnson's methods are only wasted on those who are too stupid to recognise them: 'Syllabic metres can also be recognised by ear easily enough, provided the audience is not expecting a stress metre or is prepared to pay sufficient attention to a different metrical element.'

One sentence in Johnson's 'Note on Metre' states the case more persuasively: 'Syllabic metres enable a poet to use rhythms (particularly those of colloquial speech) which are very difficult to accommodate without strain in stress metres.' This is really all that needs to be said in defence of the technique, and indeed it indicates precisely where the strengths of Johnson's poetry lie: both *Poems* and, to a greater extent, *Poems Two* (much the more relaxed and assured collection) exhibit at their best a supple command of conversational idiom, combined with an alertness to irony and a preference for tight, aphoristic forms. The language is rarely figurative; in fact in one poem, Johnson explicitly rejects such an approach on the entirely characteristic grounds that it is 'dishonest':

The sound of rain
is like only
the sound of rain

(rain seen against
the black threat
of copper beeches)

in truth can be
like nothing but
the sound of rain

'The Dishonesty of Metaphor', *Poems Two*

However, the limitations of this aesthetic are such that, in his poetry even more than in his novels, Johnson can be accused of attempting to contain experience rather than simply to render or communicate it. Often his motivation is all too visible – to take some painful event from his life and box it into verse, packaging it up into stanzas, sealing it with metre, so that its hurtful mess no longer needs to be contemplated.

Yes, I shall write it all down, you old cow,
all: the first time, the last time, all the times
in between, and then all the times I should
have liked there to have been. I shall go on
writing it down even out of habit,
till there is nothinq left to exorcise.

You may judge from that the emotional
debt I feel your lovely daughter owes me.

'Bad News for her Mother', *Poems Two*

Lines like these immediately call to mind the list of motives for writing which Johnson provided in the introduction to Aren't You Rather Young ...They included 'conceit, stubbornness, a desire to retaliate on those who have hurt me' and 'especially to exorcise, to remove from myself, from my mind, the burden [of] having to bear some pain, the hurt of some experience: in order that it may be over there, in a book, and not here in my mind .'

It's important to emphasise the aphoristic nature of Johnson's poetry. Most of his poems are extremely short, and some of them recall Ogden Nash, if anyone:

> *I'm fond of women*
> *Naked*
> *But I like my salad*
> *Dressed*

from 'Three Irrelevant Thoughts', Poems Two

The appeal of poetry for Johnson, then, would not seem to be that it offered an opportunity to write about different sorts of experience (for he used it to write about the same experiences which haunt his novels), or to write about them using language and diction in a radically different way (for he distrusted metaphor just as much in his verse as he did in his prose), but to take particular shards of experience and pin them to the page with a sort of aphoristic precision for which the novel provided little scope. 'There are certain ... experiences or certain ideas which come to me as poems,' he once said, 'and it is not an alternative to write them as a short story, or indeed as a paragraph of prose – they require the form and the rhythms and the metre of verse.' Note that emphasis on form, rhythm and metre: these, for Johnson, are the important factors.

When Bernard Bergonzi interviewed B. S. Johnson for the BBC on November 3rd, 1967 (an interview in which Johnson announced proudly that the recently published *Trawl* was 'as far as I know a hundred per cent truth as far as I could do it'), he asked him to comment on 'the relation between writing novels and writing poetry'. Johnson began his answer, as usual, by insisting upon a terminological distinction:

- Um - I'd rather make the distinction between writing novels and writing verse. It seems to me that in, at this point in

> *the Twentieth Century, as far as I'm concerned again, th ...*
> *this is a terrible conflict between you see I ... I'm really only*
> *saying what I feel and not - um - not making a general*
> *statement that applies to everyone. I feel I cannot write a*
> *long poem, that is a long piece of verse at this particular*
> *period. On the other hand I think that* Trawl *is a long poem*
> *in that it can ... it ... that it is Poetry, even though it's not in*
> *verse it's in prose. And that two hundred years ago, well*
> *this is a silly - um hypothetical statement but two hundred*
> *years ago* Trawl *would have been written in verse as a long*
> *poem, but that there are so many historical, sociological -*
> *um - temperamental reasons against writing a long poem*
> *today that I wrote it as what people call 'a novel'. That does*
> *not stop it being poetry - it is a long poem - it is not in verse,*
> *it is in prose.*

The knowledge that Johnson set so little store by the distinction between novels and poetry, then, makes us all the more keenly aware that his writing is all of a piece: just as in *Poems* and *Poems Two* we find fragments of some of the most painful incidents from his novels packaged defensively into verse, so *Trawl* and *The Unfortunates*, in particular, are best understood not as 'novels' in the neo-Dickensian sense but as poems written in prose. What unites all of his work, in whatever form, is its burning commitment to personal experience and to truth: a commitment which may have restricted Johnson in scope, but which nonetheless provoked him to ever more energetic feats of formal innovation, and so proved, in that sense, to be profoundly liberating.

CONTRIBUTORS

DAVID ALMOND's short stories have been published in numerous magazines, including *Stand, Iron* and *Bananas*, and have been broadcast on Radio 4. A collection of short stories, *Sleepless Nights*, was published by Iron Press. He edited the fiction magazine *Panurge* from 1987 to 1993. He is a regular tutor at the Arvon Foundation and the Open College of the Arts. He lives in Newcastle and works part-time in special education.

BRENDAN CLEARY lives in Newcastle upon Tyne. His latest collection, *The Irish Card*, was published by Bloodaxe.

JONATHAN COE was born in Birmingham in 1961. He now lives in London and writes regularly for a number of papers. His most recent novel is *What a Carve Up!* (Penguin)

TIM CUMMING lives in London. He has had two collections published: *The Miniature Estate* (Smith/Doorstop) and *Apocalypso* (Scratch)

JONATHAN DAVIDSON was born in south Oxfordshire in 1964. He is Director of the Birmingham Readers' and Writers' Festival. His collection *The Living Room* was published by Littlewood-Arc.

IAN DUHIG lives in Leeds and is a previous winner of the National Poetry competition. His most recent collection is *The Mersey Goldfish* (Bloodaxe)

ROBERT EDRIC lives in East Yorkshire. He is a winner of the James Tait Black Memorial Prize. His most recent books are: *Hallowed Ground* (Sunk Island Publishing) and *The Earth Made of Glass* (Picador). He recently won an Arts Council Writer's Award.

PETER FINCH was born in Cardiff and still lives there. He is a poet, short fiction writer, critic and performer. His best-sellers are *How to Publish Your Poetry* and *How to Publish Yourself* (Allison and Busby). Seren published his *Selected Poems, Poems for Ghosts* and *The Poetry Business*. He runs the Oriel Bookshop in Cardiff.

PETER HUGHES was born in 1956 and is at least half Irish. He lived in Italy from 1983 to 1991 and now teaches in a primary school near Cambridge. His most recent publications are *The Metro Poems* (Many Press, 1992) and *Psyche in the Gargano* (Equipage, 1992). These poems come from a current project inspired by the paintings and diaries of the Swiss painter Paul Klee.

DAVID LIGHTFOOT was born in Wrexham in 1941. He escaped from teaching in Lincoln to write in Louth, where he edits the poetry magazine *Seam*. His fourth poetry collection is forthcoming from Rockingham Press and his first novel, *Winterman's Company*, from Sunk Island Publishing.

BRENDON McMAHON works in a Psychotherapy Department in Derby and his poems have appeared in numerous magazines.

ED MILLER has been living and writing in the San Joaquin Valley, California for over twenty years.

GRAHAM MORT lives in North Yorkshire where he works as a freelance writer, editor and creative-writing tutor. His most recent book of poetry is *Snow from the North* (Dangaroo Press).

SEAN O'BRIEN lives in Newcastle upon Tyne. He was the Northern Arts Fellow 1992-4. In 1993 he received the *E.M. Forster Award* from the American Academy of Arts & Letters for *HMS Glasshouse* (OUP 1991). His most recent publication is *The Ghost Train* (OUP)

KEN SMITH was born in Rudston, East Yorkshire in 1938. He has worked in Britain and the USA as a freelance writer, barman, magazine editor, potato-picker and BBC reader. He lives in London. His Selected Poems, *The Poet Reclining*, was published in 1982 by Bloodaxe. A book on the fall of the Berlin Wall, *Berlin: Coming in from the Cold*. was published by Penguin in 1991. His most recent collection is *A Tender to the Queen of Spain* (Bloodaxe)

MARTIN STANNARD is a poet and reviewer. He lives in Nottinghamshire. His most recent collection is *A Hundred of Happiness* (Smith/Doorstop)

PETER TATLIN lives in London and works in publishing.